THE SECOND BURNING

PRAISE FOR TOM SCHRECK

"Schreck's unique blending of the absurd and the sublime along with his rather oddball cast of characters make his books a great read."

REED FARREL COLEMAN, TWO-TIME
SHAMUS AWARD WINNING AUTHOR
OF EMPTY EVER AFTER

"Tom Schreck will knock you to the mat with a sucker punch of laughs."

MARIO ACEVEDO, AUTHOR OF
JAILBAIT ZOMBIE

"Fresh, intense and funny."

PUBLISHERS WEEKLY

"…warmhearted, tough, funny…"

KIRKUS REVIEWS

"The writing is seamless, true artistry and a joy to read. Forget Prozac, or even that double of Bourbon, this is what feeling good is all about."

KEN BRUEN, SHAMUS AWARD-WINNING AUTHOR OF *THE GUARDS*

"Schreck is a major new talent."

JA KONRATH, AUTHOR OF *THE JACK DANIELS* SERIES

"Ten pages in, you're hooked and there's no turning back."

MICHAEL BUFFER, BOXING ANNOUNCER

"Tom Schreck delivers the grit and spit, blood and bruises of the fight game with rollicking good humor and real compassion for the underdogs among us."

SEAN CHERCOVER, AUTHOR *BIG CITY, BAD BLOOD*

"Tom Schreck is a contender for funniest author working in the crime genre today."

WILLIAM KENT KRUEGER, AUTHOR OF *VERMILION DRAFT*

THE SECOND BURNING

A FOOTBALL WEEKEND THRILLER

TRACE CURRAN THRILLER
BOOK 2

TOM SCHRECK

GLOVES OFF PUBLISHING

Library of Congress Control Number: 2026907882
Paperback ISBN: 978-1-971208-22-0
Digital Book ISBN: 978-1-971208-23-7

For my Mom and Dad.

The Great Depression kept my dad, Frank, from getting farther than the 10th grade. Every night he listened to records playing the Fight Song and he believed ND represented all that was right and good.

And for my mom, Annette, who gave me a copy of the ND student prayer book when I was in fourth grade. Mom, I still read from it every day.

Go Irish!

CHAPTER 1

George was the only one at the bar.

Actually, he wasn't alone. At his side was Rocky, my bloodhound and the official greeter at Curran's Pub.

"The Irish got Georgia this Saturday. I like their chances. I hate those SEC schools," George said. He lived and died with Notre Dame football, and his faithfulness to the bar probably had something to do with the fact that I was an alumnus.

"They cheat," George added.

"It's going to be a close game. Both teams are really good this year," I said. I tried to stay away from discussions where every college was evil except Notre Dame.

It was just after eleven, and I was busy stocking the coolers, wiping down counters, and prepping for the lunch crowd. It was late September, and the bright sunlight streaming through the windows contrasted sharply with the dark, haunted air of the old barroom.

ESPN was on in the background for white noise. It was either sports or news, and with the way politics was going these days, I couldn't bring myself to listen to the Washington talking heads. Almost as if George had cued it, the college football crew began to hype the ND-Georgia game coming up in just a few days.

"Here on the Georgia campus, the faithful are already fired up and getting ready to head north," said Ken MacAfee, the College Gameday character who was already over the top this early in the week. "We've got Earl 'Big Dog' Drummond, already so out of his mind he can't wait to get on the plane."

In front of him was an overweight, bearded fifty-something guy with a red face pumping his fists.

"Ken! The South remembers! The South remembers!" Big Dog kept repeating.

"See, Trace? Look at this asshole," George muttered.

"Well, yeah, but we've got some looney tunes cheering for the Irish too," I said, trying to take the vitriol out of George's stance.

He just shook his head and took a sip of his Miller Lite, a kind of punctuation mark before his next topic.

MacAfee kept the theme going and cut to some B-roll on the Notre Dame campus.

"And here comes the Mac the Leprechaun!" The video turned to an equally overweight, equally red-faced guy dressed in green like the ND mascot, with his gut overflowing his knickers.

"The Irish will overcome the force of red and will blarney-a-tize their chances on the gridiron!" He screamed into the camera. He said blarney-a-tize like it was in the English language.

"See, George, we got our share of looney tunes," I said.

"Theirs are worse." George was shaking his head. MacAfee changed the subject to Michigan, which came as a relief.

"No spy stuff this week?" George asked.

"No. I have to go to Washington the week after next. Just as well-I could use a break."

"Spy stuff" was George's term for my work with the CIA. I was a consulting psychologist, mostly counseling agents who'd dealt with difficult cases-terrorist acts, mass shootings, things like that. Sometimes I helped with their research efforts too. There was no point in trying to tell George I wasn't a spy.

"You miss being full-time there?" George asked.

"No. I prefer the part-time stuff. Keeps me at a safe distance," I said.

"I don't blame you-after all the shit that went down last year."

He was referring to the rogue group of terrorists who'd come after me because of something I turned up in my research. It brought terrorism to Albany-my hometown-and I didn't like thinking about it, much less talking about it.

Thankfully, my phone rang. It was Brian Hartman, my mentor from graduate school at Notre Dame.

"Trace! How the hell's the bar business?" he said with a laugh when I answered.

"Paperwork's a lot less-and so are the egos-compared to the research world," I said.

"No surprise there. How's the Agency work?"

"I still like it. Acting as a consultant makes it easier to take. The commute sucks, but getting out of this bar for a week each month is pretty therapeutic." I hesitated for a moment. "What's up-you just calling to chat?"

"No, I've got an invitation for you. The department's holding a symposium Friday on theology, antisocial behavior, and the overlap of religion and psychology. One of the panelists had to cancel, and we've got an opening. You want in?"

"This week?"

"Yeah-and there's a ticket for the Georgia game for you as well."

"Will I get introduced at halftime?"

"Of course. Come on-we'll hook up with Link and have an excuse to catch up, drink some bourbon, and talk about how we can change the world."

Link was my old roommate, best friend, and chief of campus police.

I didn't have a good reason to say no. It had been a long time since I'd set foot on campus, and despite the memories-and the skeletons in closets-I felt the pull. Plus, a ticket to the game sweetened the deal.

"Sure, why not? When do you need me there?"

"Thursday morning too soon?"

"Nah, that'll work. Can you make it so the band greets me at the airport and escorts me to campus?"

"Of course! Fight Song, On Down the Line, or The Alma Mater?"

"All three," I said.

"Done! I got you a room at the Morris Inn."

"The Morris Inn? On a football weekend against Georgia? Your rank must've gone up!"

"The symposium's part of a federal grant-we've got to spend the money!"

"See you Thursday," I said.

I put my phone in my pocket. George was staring at me.

"You're going to the game?" he said.

"Yes, sir!"

"Hot dog! Good for you!" he said.

"Go Irish!" I said, pumping my fist.

CHAPTER 2

There's something about going back to a place where you went from a kid to an almost man that brings a ton of emotion. I mean, I was seventeen when I went to college, had never been away from home for more than a night, and suddenly I was someplace where I didn't know a soul. Four years later, I felt on top of the world-and somewhat scared about leaving the safety and nurturing of that same place.

Of course, all of this blends into the lore and legend that make Notre Dame so powerful. It's part the place, the history, and the values-and part the fact that you experience it as a kid, and then maybe as a man-child at best. When you look back, it all comes together in a cloud of romantic nostalgia that blurs over the awkward and painful, leaving you with the warmth of having done something special.

You put a big golden dome in the middle of the place, beautiful grounds, and spiritual references every five feet, and it gets inside you-becomes part of you.

I still had to get there. That meant an early morning

flight to Chicago's Midway, a rental car, and an eighty-minute ride through eastern Illinois and northern Indiana. The drive had some new sights-casinos and developments-and some that had gone away, like Charles O. Finley's barn with the big gothic "A" on top, he being the owner of the Oakland Athletics.

Then there were some that would never change, like the orange skyline of Gary. It was hard not to think about Michael Jackson and how he got from such a hellish place to where he did.

A smile crossed my face when I passed the Knute Rockne Rest Stop on the toll road. It brought back memories of the continuous showings of *Knute Rockne, All American* that ran from noon to midnight during freshman orientation. Shouts of "Don't get on the plane, Knute!" were part of the experience-and one of those things you just wouldn't get at the University at Albany.

The sign for South Bend, Notre Dame, and St. Mary's College ignited a rush of excitement, and I could feel that old tingle of expectation as I hit the exit. Coming around the big sweeping arterial off the toll road put you right in the center of a nearly perfect side view of the Golden Dome and the Basilica. My eyes were only half on the road as the Dome gleamed in the gray, overcast sky that South Bend seemed to live under eighty percent of the time.

It was a football week-and not just any football week. It was the Irish against Georgia from George's evil SEC, and the traffic showed how big the game was, even though it was early morning two full days before kickoff. When I made the left down Notre Dame Avenue, with the Golden Dome framed at the end by the tree-lined road-the cemetery that held Knute for eternity on the left, DeBartolo Quad on the right, and the massive stadium looming behind-I couldn't help but smile. Memories and pride filled me, along with a ton of gratitude that I got to be part of this place.

The Morris Inn-no longer the same Morris Inn from my student days-was a left turn right before the Hammes Bookstore, already jam-packed with the faithful throwing down thousands to get just the right Irish gear. Across from it stood Alumni Hall, deemed "The Center of the Universe" by those who lived there, and the place I'd spent my undergraduate years. Its gargoyles and the bust of Rockne's dog, Clashmore Mike-ND's first mascot before they went with the leprechaun-still stood proudly. Next to Alumni was its hated rival, Dillon Hall, filled with guys who'd seen *Animal House* too many times and fancied themselves something special.

It was the job of Alumni residents to remind them they weren't.

Entering the Morris Inn the week of a big game meant walking through a lobby populated with Notre Dame's elite-anointed and sainted. I pulled my carry-on to the front desk, and in terms of the kind of Domer you could bump into, I hit the jackpot.

Joe Montana.Joe *Freakin'* Montana.

I let him and his wife check in, and the front desk clerk seemed to expedite the process for blue-and-gold royalty-as they should. As he turned and I took his place in line, our eyes met briefly.

"Hey Joe," I said, trying to sound nonchalant. "Thanks."

"Hey, how's it going?" Joe said before heading to the

elevator-if not at a hurried pace, at least a brisk one. He didn't ask me what I was thanking him for.

He knew.

I got my room key and headed for the elevator. Waiting there were Ian Book and Jerome "The Bus" Bettis, whose son was on the current team. I knew I was grinning like an idiot as the three of us stepped into the elevator together.

"Go Irish," I said, using the official greeting that helped reduce the stupid fanboy comments one is likely to blurt in front of their heroes.

Ian and The Bus returned the greeting.

I could die a happy man now.

I skipped the nap I'd promised myself because I had to walk around campus. I especially wanted to experience it while the university was in full swing-mid-morning on a Thursday. The students looked way too young to be in college, and it brought back the feeling of being young myself, before life gave me reasons for cynicism.

I headed down the South Quad, past Dillon and South Dining Hall, to the Rockne Memorial, then turned past Morrissey and Lyons Halls, cut down the sidewalk by the Knights of Columbus, and made my way toward the Grotto.

The Grotto was my most cherished part of campus. It sits below the Golden Dome where the two lakes-St. Joseph's and St. Mary's-come together. It's a replica of the Grotto at Lourdes, where the Virgin Mother appeared to three little girls. It would be busy today, the Thursday before a big game, and finding a spot for a candle would be tough.

During my time here, I came to the Grotto most days. I'd

kneel and try to pray, though my mind often struggled with the process. I'd pick a spot near the encased letter from Dr. Tom Dooley to Father Hesburgh, where Dooley wrote how often he cherished his Grotto memories while treating sick children in the Far East.

I came down the hill with St. Mary's Lake and Holy Cross Hall in front of me, but before I could turn toward the Grotto, my reverie was shattered when someone grabbed me from behind and squeezed like they wanted me to explode.

"What the-oh shit-" I half-yelled. I was released, turned around, and there he was: my old dorm mate Link-short for Lincoln Christian-the current chief of campus police.

"Damn, you're easy, bro," he said with a laugh.

Link was a legacy, but of a different kind. His Irish Catholic mom was one of the first women admitted in 1972. His dad was an African American non-athlete, which was pretty rare back then. Link had walked on and played for the football prep team. With his fade haircut, strong jawline, and maybe eight percent body fat, he looked just about the same as he had in school. When we got drunk, we used to call him "Chocolate Rudy" because of his prep team stint. He was the middleweight Bengal Bouts champ his Junior and Senior year while I was still doing Tae Kwon Do.

Standing next to him, actually more like seven or eight feet back was a short, thin black girl, probably a student. She stood with her hands folded in front of her, a smart phone in her bottom hand.

"You're lucky I don't get a lawyer and sue you-and Our Lady's university-for police brutality!" I said, sticking out my hand before we hugged.

"I heard you got added to some egghead symposium. What are you pontificating on tomorrow-'Why Criminals Are Bad?'"

"Exactly," I said, shaking my head. "Look, in my continuing effort to be holier than thou, I was headed to the Grotto to beg forgiveness for the things we yelled out the windows at Dillon."

Link paused for a second.

"Oh, Trace, excuse me," He paused kind of awkwardly. "This is Jo Pierre. She's a student doing work study in my office."

I extended my hand to her. "Go Irish!" I said.

She frowned and looked down before saying:

"Pleasure to meet you." It was not quite formal. More perfunctory.

"You like the Irish's chances tomorrow?" I said.

She frowned again.

"Uh, Jo's not a huge football gal," Link said.

Just then, the sound of a loud, severely out-of-tune band echoed through campus-tubas, trombones, trumpets, gongs-not the Band of the Fighting Irish. Firecrackers, whistles...the sounds of chaos.

"The Viking Parade?" I asked, knowing full well.

"Geez, I hate this shit." And as director of campus police, I could understand why. The men of Zahm Hall had a tradition of dressing up like Vikings-and cavemen, pagans, gorillas-and picking random times to march through campus. The university had closed Zahm a couple of years ago, if that tells you anything. The parade was usually during big-game week, but part of the "fun" was its unpredictability. Just a couple of hundred young Domers marching around creating noise, smoke, and utter nonsense.

Except now there was no Zahm. A bunch of old guys from the Zahm of the '70s had brought back the Viking Parade. Picture sixty- and seventy-year-olds doing this in public for fun.

"The Vikings gave us notice they'll be doing their shit all weekend. No schedule-just whenever their blood-alcohol percentage hits the magic number," Link said. "ESPN is here to document their existence."

"Ahhh, tradition..." I said.

Link's phone rang.

"What? Above the grotto? I'm on my way."

He wasn't smiling anymore.

"What's going on?" I asked, suddenly serious.

"There's a dead body in the garden between the grotto and the Basilica."He turned and started running past the Grotto and up the stairs toward the garden. Jo fell in behind him.

CHAPTER 3

Link was in a full cop wind sprint.I didn't know what to do. My short trip back to my alma mater had instantly gone from a nostalgic, dreamlike excursion to something else. My idyllic, coming-of-age *Wizard of Oz* moment had just turned into something sinister.

Instead of a prayerful meditation at the Grotto, I jogged past it, noting the usual gatherings of people lighting candles and kneeling in prayer. It didn't feel right to run past a place so dear to me, but I felt like I needed to be with Link. I went around the Grotto and up the steep hill that led to the sidewalk between the Golden Dome and the Basilica.

Behind the Basilica, six campus police officers and Link were forming a barrier circle around a body. It was an isolated part of campus wedged between the Golden Dome, the Basilica, and the Grotto in a quiet niche that could be easily missed by someone who hadn't spent a lot of time on campus.

An ambulance pulled up the same access road next to the Grotto only a minute or two after me. Whether their efficiency was about trying to save the man's life or about minimizing a public-relations nightmare for the university was open to cynical conjecture. The police surrounded the body, giving the EMTs a few feet to work it onto the stretcher and to keep onlookers away. In moments, the ambulance was on its way, heading across the road that led to Highway 31 and the St. Mary's College campus.

By now, the South Bend Police and the Indiana State Police had arrived, and a cluster of them had formed around Link, who seemed to be doing all the talking. Jo stood off from the circle of cops and was entering something into her phone. The other campus police barely interacted with the SBP or ISP. My limited experience with law enforcement told me that the usual turf issues were going to be a thing.

A forensic team began their work where the body had been. A crude chalk outline on the sidewalk just above the grotto stood in contrast to the sacred place just below. A facilities crew from the university waited, if not patiently, with a power washer. A bloody murder scene and a chalk outline weren't what the powers that be wanted visitors to see this weekend.

Because of the location, neither fans nor students had gathered. That was a public relations break for the university.

The forensic team collected whatever they needed, packed it into their van, and nodded to their supervisors. The lead investigator spoke to Link, and Link gave a nod to the facilities crew-who wasted no time firing up the power washer to erase all evidence of what had occurred. Within minutes, all that remained was a wet sidewalk.

Forty-five minutes later, with notebooks full of whatever cops write, the South Bend and State Police packed up and left. Link talked to his officers, who then dispersed to their usual posts across campus-probably breaking up kids who'd gotten an early start on tomorrow's tailgating.

Link spotted me standing near the Basilica, trying to look inconspicuous.

"I'm gonna have to spend some time with the paperwork and call the president," he said. "After that, I'm going to need a beer."

"Call me when you're ready," I said.

He nodded.

"Jo, you get this?" Link moved his head from side to side signalling for her to record everything she could.

I headed back to my room at the Morris Inn. The northern Indiana sky had darkened, and it started to rain lightly at first-but by the time I passed Walsh Hall and was approaching Alumni, the skies opened up. I hunched my shoulders and quickened my pace as I hurried past Clashmore Mike. His mood seemed to have changed along with mine-and the weather.

I hadn't even been here for a full day yet.

What the hell just happened?

CHAPTER 4

I'd gone back to the Morris Inn for a shower and thought I might nap a little. It had already been a long day even without the incident-an early flight, the airport hassle, the rental car, the drive from Chicago, the excitement of being on campus-and then, damn, a murder. There was no nap to be had; too much adrenaline was still running through my veins.

Instead, I walked the campus. It was dark now, with a misty rain falling on my ND baseball cap-the traditional one I preferred, navy blue with the interlocking ND. I stayed mostly dry in my windbreaker hoodie from the Crawford YMCA Boxing Club, a gift from my fight buddy, Duffy, back home.

I wandered the campus, listening to the music blaring from the dorms. It used to be Springsteen, The Who, the Grateful Dead, maybe some ironic Journey or The Cars. Now it was Luke Bryan, Kenny Chesney, and a handful of other country rockers who all sounded the same to me.

In the distance, the Irish band was marching back to

their building, kicking into the fight song before calling it a night-a night followed by a quick turnaround to get the campus pumping for the Georgia Bulldogs tomorrow and early Saturday. Back in my day, the band started the fight song right outside Alumni Hall before marching out to Green Field for practice. To be honest, as cynical as I could get, I never tired of hearing it. It reminded me of my dad and how important this place was to a guy who never got the chance to go to college.

It dawned on me that, with everything that had happened, I hadn't given much thought to my panel symposium. That was probably okay. As a psychologist, I was used to pontificating with big words. Panels weren't hard-there'd be others at the table who loved hearing the sound of their own voices even more than I did.

I found myself near the stadium, in front of the Lou Holtz statue, when my phone rang.

"You up for a beer?" It was Link.

"Have I ever not been?" I said.

"Sophomore year, when you puked from all the shots. You took a week off."

"True."

"Legends in about twenty minutes?"

"Isn't that going to be mobbed? Wall-to-wall Domers in brand-new quarter-zips?"

"You realize you're talking to the Chief of Campus Police, don't you? I've commandeered one of the private rooms."

"Big shot," I said.

"See you in twenty." He hung up.

It used to be that Legends was the senior bar-a run-down house on the edge of campus through the '70s and early '80s. Now, Legends had all the charm of a Buffalo Wild Wings and let anyone in. Gone were the days when you had to flash your ND class ring to prove you were a student-and, more importantly, a senior.

The doorman was a campus security cop, not a beefy third third-string lineman trying to look menacing. That's who worked the door in my day.

"Link asked me to meet him," I said as I walked to the front of the line.

"You Trace?"

I nodded.

"Follow me."

We waded through a sea of Notre Dame humanity-made easier by my escort-until we reached the back wall and a door marked *Employees Only.* The cop opened it with a key, and inside a small meeting room-probably meant for staff lunches or private gatherings-was Link. A pitcher of beer and two pint glasses sat on the table.

"Wings and pizza are on the way," he said.

"Has the food here gotten any better?" I asked.

"Absolutely not." He poured beers for both of us. "Sit down. I've got to pry into your highly developed CIA psychology mind."He slid a manila envelope my way.

It was a series of photographs from the crime scene.

"I thought the staties would've taken over," I said.

"Oh, make no mistake-they have. But this is still my campus."

"Father Sorin notwithstanding." I paused. "Not sure this is the kind of thing you wanted to be known for, but this has to be the first murder on campus ever."

"Actually, it isn't. In '75, Helen Toboloski, a custodial worker, was murdered in the early morning hours in the aerospace building."

"Really?"

"Yeah, it's not talked about alot. It was never solved." Link shrugged and tapped on the manila envelope.

"Hey, before I look at all of this–what's the deal with, uh, your number two there, your assistant? What was it? Jo?"

Link chuckled to himself

"She's a trip, isn't she?" He half laughed. "Brilliant. Electrical Engineering/Biology double major."

"Slacker." I said. "Not exactly Lou Holtz when it comes to school spirit."

"No, she has no desire to smack the Play like a Champions" sign at all." Link paused. "But I get it."

"Huh?"

Link let out a breath.

"You've seen those "What would you fight for?" videos they show at the games and during commercials?"

"Sure, they make me cry." I said only half kidding.

"Ever see the one on Haiti?" Link raised his eyebrows.

"Yeah…"

"Remember the woman with the elephantitis in her legs?"

"Yeah, brutal."

Link paused.

"That's Jo's mom. Her dad and three brothers died in the earthquake. Students, faculty and Holy Cross fathers worked with the family. They got Jo into a high school and got her tutoring."

"Holy shit…" I said.

"Yeah, Notre Dame isn't about football and keggers for her. They saved her mom's life. They saved her life." Link took a second. "She's studying to go back there and help."

"Jesus…"

"3.96 GPA. 20 credits a semester and work study. She argued with a sociology prof about poverty and he gave her an A minus. The only time I saw her rattled." He looked down at the folder on the table and handed it to me.

The photos showed the victim. The first was a facial close-up, probably for identification. The next showed the positioning of the body from about eight feet away. Then came close-ups of the wounds,wounds and then of each hand. One hand held a bead of some sort. Another shot showed a singed piece of paper.

"What am I looking for?" I asked.

He pointed to the hands. "His right hand is clenched. His left hand is open, palm up. A single rosary bead in it. It is burnt."

I looked closer. "Looks like it was placed," I said.

"That's what I thought. And the body was found just above the grotto."

I sat back. "So someone staged this."

"Yeah. The dead guy is a Holy Cross father. Father Lucas Bellamy. He's a priest and a professor of theology. His main thrust is on the immorality of racism and xenophobia."

"A Holy Cross Father, I guess that's not too surprising. They still run the place," I said.

"He was here to be on a panel about racism, theology, and psychology."

"Hold it-that's the panel I'm on."

"Exactly," Link said.

I didn't like where this was going.

"Anything on motive?"

Link shook his head. "No wallet. No phone. Nothing missing. But get this-on the sidewalk, chalked just outside the body outline, someone wrote: *The Agony in the Garden*."

My stomach dropped. "The first of the Sorrowful Mysteries?"

Link nodded. "That's what Campus Ministry confirmed."

"What's with the piece of paper?" I asked.

"It was in his suit coat. Only thing on him-no wallet, no keys, just this."

"It's parchment," he said. "Looks very old or made to look very old. I'm checking with Special Collections at the library."

"What's it say?"

"There's a lot of mumbo-jumbo-sounds like some sort of graduation tribute or dedication. Not sure of the significance. But check out this line near the bottom:

Let the fires of Atlanta speak for eternity. They are not embers of war, but of reckoning..."

"I don't think that's from Kirby Smart," I said.

"Weird coincidence if it has something to do with the game."

"Weird is right," I said. "And scary."

CHAPTER 5

After more beers and conversation, Link backed off hanging out any longer,citing the fact that it was Thursday night and the next two days were going to be busy. I got back to my room, but sleep wasn't going to come easily. I poured myself a bourbon, propped up some pillows, and tried to use the TV as sleep medication. Despite DirecTV's five thousand channels, the only things that interested me were *SportsCenter* or *Forensic Files.* I'd had my fill of forensics for the day, so I chose sports.

Not surprisingly, the focus was on the game to be played less than two days from now-about a five-minute walk from where I was sipping Knob Creek in my undershorts. Coach Freeman was doing his interview and, as always, handling it with class, confidence, and grace.

"Coach, you're the only Black head coach to have played in the national championship game. How does that feel?" came the question from Reece Davis.

"Well, I'm very proud of my heritage as both an African American and a Korean American. Still, the focus is on this university and the young men who are working so hard to represent it." Coach Freeman never appeared rattled when questions like that came up-and Lord knows, he'd had plenty of practice.

Next, they shifted to the betting lines, outlining that the Irish were a 3.5-point underdog. The question was whether ND's new quarterback would be up for a game of this magnitude. Sure, he'd had great starts against Miami and Texas A&M, but Georgia-especially this year-was something else entirely. Like playing on national television every week, in hostile stadiums, under constant media scrutiny, and with the pressure of the Notre Dame faithful wasn't enough to toughen a guy up.

Then they cut to the knucklehead Georgia fan-red face paint, sweatshirt with an oversized Uga bulldog on his chest-yelling into the camera.

"The South remembers!" he shouted. Then they cut to Mac the leprechaun. "God made whiskey so the Irish wouldn't conquer the world!" Mac yelled. Great, score another one for stereotypes. Geez.

The football distraction didn't induce sleep-it had the opposite effect. My mind drifted back to the murder and to my alma mater. Being on campus does that to you. You come expecting nostalgia-the retelling of great stories, drunken adolescent nonsense, bad dates, dining hall hijinks. Yeah, you get that-but you also get the memories of stress, heartbreak, and the awkwardness of trying to be both a grown-up and a carefree kid at the same time. There were the football weekends, the Dome, the Grotto-but there was also the real stuff of coming of age.

It wasn't all fun, though that's what you remember when you head back.

It was college-and not everyone navigated it well. There was a guy on our floor, a scholarship athlete, who went home in October and never came back. Talk was he'd had a breakdown, a psychiatric stay, and the crushing of all the dreams he'd carried up until then. He wasn't the only one.

Then there was the drinking. We all drank too much-but some guys were drinking for different reasons, and they didn't shake it off once Sunday morning came around. There were incidents-like at all colleges, with this age group and that much alcohol-things that weren't flattering, and I'm sure left people scarred for life.

Memories of college-including Notre Dame-tend to airbrush the background.

I got out of bed and stood by the window. The rain had thinned to a mist. The glow of the Dome in the distance made the sky look backlit by something holy. Mix in the emotions of returning here-with a murder thrown in-and I wasn't sure what I was thinking or feeling.

Whoever staged the priest's murder didn't just want to kill him. They wanted to say something. The line about Atlanta was bizarre-sounded like a sermon disguised as a warning.

When I'd been a psych grad student pulling all-nighters in the library, I'd survived on coffee and librarians-especially one, Jane Harris. She was the kind of research librarian who didn't just find what you were looking for; she found what you didn't know you needed. It was late, but I had to reach out.

I texted her, not expecting a reply:*Sorry to bug you so late.*

Need help tracking a doc. Might be Civil War-era, might be something else. Any chance you're still up?

She replied two minutes later:

You always were better at questions than deadlines. Meet me at the library at 9 tomorrow morning. I know someone.

The next morning, the campus felt half-awake. Rain gave everything a reflective sheen. Undergrads shuffled in hoodies, coffee cups clutched like relics. The campus already had that game-week buzz, amplified by the presence of ESPN's *College GameDay.* They were setting up like a state fair halfway between the north end of the stadium and the library-angled so "Touchdown Jesus," the grand mosaic looming over the end zone, would fill the background of every shot.

"Touchdown Jesus" was what fans called it. The official name was The Word of Life; for students, it was the library- or "The 'Brar." Twelve stories high, it was one of the largest university libraries in the country, home to some of the most extensive collections anywhere. To undergrads, though, it was mostly known for its second-floor study area-a place that gathered hundreds each night and was probably the least effective spot to study on campus.

I entered through the side by the Moses statue. Jane was already there, perched behind the reference desk like she'd never left it. Glasses on a beaded chain, sharp-eyed, not one to waste time on small talk.

She smiled-barely. "Thomas Eberly," she said, gesturing toward a tall, skinny thirty-something with a man bun, thin beard, and wire-rimmed glasses. He wore a flannel shirt and cargo pants, hunched over a folio like it contained the secrets of the universe.

"Dr. Eberly manages our Civil War archives in Special Collections," Jane said. "If what you've got is from then-or close to it-he'll know."

I handed him a copy of the parchment photo. His eyes lit up the way only archivists' and certain fanatics' eyes can.

"Fascinating," he murmured. "Where did you get this?"

"Off a murdered priest."

He blinked. "Ah." He looked back at the photo. "This is clearly designed to resemble the 1865 commencement address given by General Tecumseh Sherman."

"General Sherman-the Civil War Sherman? He gave the commencement address?"

"In 1865, right after the war ended. His family lived on campus." Eberly clearly enjoyed being the expert.

"They did?" I said.

"The university played a significant role in the war. Over forty Holy Cross fathers served as chaplains. Father Corby gave the troops last rites before the battle at Appomattox."

I was dumbfounded. "Hold it. Didn't Sherman burn Atlanta?" A chill ran through me.

"All of Georgia-and much of every state he passed through. Then he burned South Carolina."

"Not hard to see why Notre Dame isn't popular in the South," I said. Eberly gave me a half-hearted, patronizing smile.

"Now this," he said, pointing to the photograph, "is something else entirely. It's made to look like Sherman's speech, but it's not. The language is different."

"But it's written in his style?"

"It mimics him, yes. But this isn't authentic. Whoever

wrote it either fabricated it or uncovered an obscure forgery."

"And Bellamy? Could he have been working on this?"

Eberly tapped his chin. "He came to the archives last week. Requested access to our Civil War theological texts-things most people don't ask for unless they're deep into niche studies. Said he was investigating 'misused wartime sermons' and didn't elaborate."

I nodded, thanked them both, and walked outside.

The rain had stopped. The clouds were breaking. If someone thought they were reenacting the Stations of the Cross-with a fake Sherman text as scripture-this wasn't just about theology.

It was about history. And maybe vengeance.

CHAPTER 6

I sat looking at the photo of the parchment. A document meant to be mistaken for General Tecumseh Sherman? An alternative commencement address that he thought better of? And above all-why? After all, it had been a few years since the Civil War, and we had moved on.

Or, I'd like to believe, most of us had.

So, this priest, who had, the best I could tell, lived a very uncontroversial life, got choked out, posed, and planted with a burnt rosary bead and a Civil War relic.

Why?

Was this about murder, or was this about some twisted message?

I was pretty sure, being the genius that I am, that it was a message.

The body was found on top of the grotto. Not just dumped, but presented. Like a statement or a warning, but what were we being warned about? And during the week of this year's game of the century.

I made my way back to the Main Building. I didn't exactly feel like I had a purpose; it was more like a wandering curiosity. It was the day before a huge game, and the campus energy was building, but it was still early in the day for it to reach its full tilt frenzy. Walsh Hall had a series of bed sheets turned into banners celebrating the game. One depicted the Leprechaun stealing Uga, the bulldog who was UGA's mascot; another read, "The Irish have Touchdown Jesus, UGA has Touchdown GED."

I still liked when ND played Navy ahead of USC on the schedule. "First the Seamen, then the Trojans!" was tough to beat.

Of course, the nice ladies of Walsh would probably avoid that one unless things at ND had changed... a lot.

Everyone had heard about the body by now. Heinous murders weren't a Notre Dame thing. Notre Dame doesn't do murders-not on the quad, not during Georgia week, and definitely not in front of the Blessed Mother.

I headed to the Theology Department's makeshift symposium suite-a couple of borrowed offices and a conference room on the third floor of O'Shaughnessy Hall. Bellamy had been using a shared adjunct office for the week. Campus security had probably swept it already, but they knew I had a different kind of access. Sometimes, it's not what you know-it's what people think you know.

Unlike the Grotto, the Dome, or the Stadium, O'Shag Hall brought back a different type of nostalgia. Three-hour lectures, no air conditioning, required seminars in Comp & Lit, and six theology credits. For a 19-year-old, it was a bit hard to have a true appreciation of the depth of the educational opportunities in front of me at age 18. There were more important things to think about, like 50-cent beer nights at The Commons and that brunette who lived in McCandless over at SMC who seemed to return my glance the week before.

The door wasn't locked. Inside was organized academic clutter: open folders, sticky notes, coffee-stained papers. One book caught my eye: *Scars of Redemption: Sacrifice and Retribution in American Sermons, 1776-1945.*

Then Bellamy's folder-highlighted: *"Righteous Fire: The Sermon as Moral Weapon."*

And a single handwritten sheet:

"The Via Dolorosa - Twelve Steps to Salvation Through Suffering"

Below that, a list:

1. Condemnation
2. The Burden Accepted
3. Collapse of Flesh
4. The Watchers
5. Simon's Strength
6. Comfort of the Veil...

It wasn't Bellamy's sermon. It was... a *record*. Notes on someone else's warped framework.

At the bottom, scrawled: *"Dangerous?"* and *"Second Burning-ritualized violence? Must alert Lacey."*

I exhaled. Bellamy wasn't the zealot here-he'd uncovered one.

The door creaked behind me.

"Trace?"

It was Brian.

"Didn't expect to see you here this early," he said. "The symposium isn't until this afternoon."

"I was hoping to get a read on Bellamy's state of mind."

I showed him the sheet.

Hartman frowned. "That's not his theology. He'd been worried. Said someone was twisting liturgical history-obsessed with sacrifice and suffering."

"Who?"

Hartman shrugged.

"Bellamy was trying to stop him," I said.

"And got himself killed," Hartman replied.

I pointed to the note about Reverend Lacey. "You know anything about this?"

Brian nodded. "Visiting theology professor from Mercer. They butted heads at the planning meeting. Bellamy accused him of theological sanitizing-said Lacey had scrubbed violence from wartime liturgies. Suggested he was disguising his racism in theology.Lacey didn't take it well."

"Where do I find him?"

"He's got an office downstairs. Or he'll be at the panel walkthrough in an hour."

"I'll find him."

I tracked Reverend Anthony Lacey to a chapel lounge near the south side of campus. The moment he saw me, I could tell he knew who I was.

"If this is about Bellamy," he said, "I've already spoken to campus police."

"I'm not the police."

"That's worse." He motioned for me to sit.

Lacey was in his sixties, pressed black suit, modest rep tie, who had mastered the stern-but-kind look. He folded his hands.

"Father Bellamy had... radical ideas," he said. "He was theologically disingenuous."

"What does that even mean?" I said.

"He had used theology to explain his woke philosophy. It was disingenuous."

"What about General Sherman?"

Lacey tilted his head. "What about him?"

"What was his significance to Father Bellamy...or to you?"

"Sherman's march would be considered a war crime today. He was a criminal." Lacey's face was expressionless, but his eyes looked at me with intensity.

I stood. "Thank you, Reverend. I'll see you at the panel."

"You will?"

"Yes, I'm a psychologist. My topic is terrorism and how it is justified."

He snorted in mock laughter and returned his gaze to the volume in front of him.

My phone pinged.

Link texted: *Need you at the Grotto. Now.*

I sprinted across campus, heart already ahead of me.

The Stations of the Cross start behind Columba Hall, across from the Grotto. The path circles St. Joseph's Lake, and every fifty feet or so, there's a modest wooden post with a plaque marking one of the stations. At the end stands a breathtaking bronze crucifix on a small hill just off the path. It was a gift from a woman in France more than

150 years ago, and it inspires awe in the truest sense of the word. The Stations are usually a quiet spot for prayer and reflection.

Except today.

I'm a psychologist, and though I consult with the CIA and other government entities, that doesn't mean I'm used to seeing this kind of trauma up close. Honestly, I wanted to help Link, and I didn't like anyone disturbing my alma mater-but all of this was starting to turn my stomach. I knew what trauma was; it's been my life's work. But that didn't make me immune to it.

I felt that distant, dissociated feeling that comes with it.

I reached the scene just in time to watch them zip up the bag with the victim inside. Link was in the center of the activity. State police stood everywhere, both in uniform and plainclothes. South Bend PD was there too. A lot of people were doing what law enforcement often does-standing around, waiting for orders. An ambulance finally pulled away with the body.

I approached Link but didn't interrupt his official business. He spotted me and gave a quick nod, then hurried over. Jo was there, keeping the same distance I'd seen before.

"At the crucifix," Link pointed his head in the direction of the bronze statue that came at the end of the Stations of the Cross. "This was with it."

He handed me a note.

"The Crowning of Thorns. You will recognize the image of false authority before the fire."

I read it through several times.

"What the hell does this mean?"

Link shrugged.

"It is the third of the Sorrowful Mysteries." Jo said, trying to be unobtrusive.

Link had said she was devout. I hadn't looked at my Catechism in awhile.

"Who was the victim?" I asked.

Link raised his eyebrows.

"Get this. Professor at UGA. Her ID says sociology department. She had this on her."

Link handed me a trifold brochure.

"DEI: Its Implications for Today's Corporations." It was a seminar scheduled for Monday at the Mendoza School of Business. Notre Dame's business school was tops in the country.

"DEI," I repeated.

"Yeah," Link said. "Might be a coincidence."

"Or we might have a crazy racist murderer on campus a day before the biggest game in years."

"I was trying not to think like that," Link said. His face was tight.

Link left to confer with the circle of investigators. It would be hours before he could talk again. After fifteen minutes, the writing was on the wall-I had to leave. I still had a couple of hours before the symposium and needed to do something. What, I wasn't sure.

Like every good PhD, that meant going back to the library. I'd spent so much time there over my twelve years at Notre Dame that it felt as familiar as any living room I'd ever had. I long ago dismissed the second-floor social crowd and spent most of my time in the Special Archives section, open to me because of my degree. The ten-minute walk let me think, though my thoughts were fogged by everything happening.

Jane was at the circulation desk when I arrived. She always was-steady as the mosaic of Jesus, the Word of Life-better known to ESPN heads as "Touchdown Jesus."

"I don't see you for five years, and now I see you twice in one morning?" Jane said, skipping a second greeting.

"Yeah. There's been another death. Down by the Stations near the Grotto." There was no easy way to say it. My gut twisted as the words came out.

"Oh my God." Jane put a hand to her chest. "What is going on?"

"No one knows." I hesitated. "Could I look at the archives on Sherman-his commencement speech and any theological material from the Civil War era?"

"Sure. Come with me."

I followed Jane around the stacks and through a glass door into a space known as Special Collections. It was part of what made the Hesburgh Library academically renowned. She stopped before a set of shelves, scanning for something.

"It's usually right here, in this section," she murmured. "The Sherman volumes." She turned and spotted it. "Oh-here it is."

Jane grabbed a file from the "To Be Shelved" cart.

"Here, Trace. Knock yourself out."

She handed me a three-inch bound manuscript of photocopies and notes from Sherman's writings. Some were in his own hand; others had typed transcriptions and photographs of the general, his children, and Mrs. Sherman.

An   abstract   opened   the   volume,   summarizing

Sherman's role in the war and his relationship with the university. It read:

The Civil War Legacy of General William Tecumseh Sherman and His Relationship with the University of Notre Dame

General William Tecumseh Sherman remains one of the most formidable and controversial figures of the American Civil War. As commander of Union forces in the western theater, Sherman orchestrated the infamous March to the Sea in late 1864, which began with the siege and burning of Atlanta. His campaign employed scorched-earth tactics aimed at crippling the Confederate war effort and breaking the morale of the Southern population. The systematic destruction of railroads, factories, plantations, and civilian property left a legacy of bitterness across the former Confederacy-sentiments that, in some quarters, have endured to the present day.

Sherman's personal connections to the University of Notre Dame and the Congregation of Holy Cross present an intriguing dimension to his public legacy. Several of Sherman's children were educated in South Bend: his eldest son, Thomas Ewing Sherman, enrolled at Notre Dame and later became a Jesuit priest; his daughter, Eleanor ("Ellie"), attended Saint Mary's College. Sherman himself developed a strong personal friendship with Father Edward Sorin, founder of Notre Dame. Their correspondence reflects shared admiration, a commitment to education, and a vision of national healing after the war.

In 1865, soon after the end of hostilities, Sherman delivered a commencement address at Notre Dame. His speech celebrated perseverance, sacrifice, and moral duty, while warning that the scars of civil conflict would endure for generations. Sherman praised the role of the Holy Cross fathers, whose chaplains had served with distinction in the Union Army. The university's wartime loyalty to the Union, combined with its postwar embrace of Northern leaders like Sherman, became an indelible part of Notre Dame's institutional identity.

This intertwining of Sherman's legacy with Notre Dame - a Northern Catholic university with deep Civil War roots - continues to shape perceptions of the institution's place in American history. For some, it is a symbol of reconciliation. For others, it remains a reminder of old divisions and unhealed wounds.

After reading the summary, I flipped to Sherman's 1865 commencement address, curious to see what the general had said about the war and the university.

"Young gentlemen of Notre Dame,

The past four years have tested this nation beyond measure. Brother has stood against brother; cities have burned; brave men have fallen on every field from the Potomac to the Mississippi.

Yet from this crucible we emerge, if not unscathed, then wiser. You - the students of this great Catholic institution - have been spared the direct horrors of the battlefield. But you are inheritors of its lessons.

The service of the Holy Cross fathers as chaplains and healers upon those bloody fields stands as a beacon of faith amid the fire of war. Let this inspire you: that sacrifice in the name of unity, of moral right, of our common humanity, is not wasted.

War is a dreadful thing - I pray you shall never know it. Yet there are times when evil must be opposed, and division must be healed not by words alone, but by resolute action.

The fires of Atlanta, though terrible, were not kindled in cruelty, but in grim necessity. So too must the fires of learning, of piety, and of national brotherhood now burn brighter - so this republic may know peace.

Go forth, then, armed not with sword or rifle, but with conscience, wisdom, and faith. The true test of this generation will not be what was destroyed - but what shall be built in its place."

It went on from there with more of the same rhetoric. Nothing I could find that would ignite anything even in an extremist's mind.

Then I came across this:

The So-Called "Second Burning" Sherman Address - Origins and Context

Among the more troubling documents to surface in extremist circles in recent years is a text often referred to as the "Second Burning" address - a revisionist, incendiary version of General William Tecumseh Sherman's well-documented 1865 commencement speech at the University of Notre Dame.

The original address, preserved in Notre Dame's archives, was a call for reconciliation, moral reflection, and national healing. It praised the role of the Holy Cross fathers during the war and urged the new generation of American youth toward civic virtue and unity.

The "Second Burning" text, by contrast, is an anonymous,

undated polemic that perverts Sherman's language into a pseudo-theological justification for violence and racialist revenge. It first appeared in fragmentary form in online forums frequented by neo-Confederate and white nationalist groups in the early 2000s, though internal references suggest it may have circulated in some form during the late 20th century.

No original handwritten copy has been authenticated. Scholars generally consider it a deliberate forgery - crafted not to deceive historians but to inspire modern extremist ideology by evoking the imagery of Sherman's march and the destruction of Atlanta. The text's repeated references to "fire," "cleansing," and "Second Burning" align with themes of martyrdom and retribution common in far-right rhetoric.

Of particular note is its targeting of Notre Dame itself - portraying the university as complicit in a supposed betrayal of Southern honor through its Union loyalties and friendship with Sherman. While the true authorship of the forged address remains unknown, it has served as a touchstone for contemporary extremists seeking to mythologize the Civil War through a lens of grievance, religious distortion, and anti-Catholic paranoia.

It was part of the burned parchment found in Bellamy's hand.

What the hell?

Jane's voice broke my trance.

"Find anything interesting?"

"You know anything about the *Second Sherman Commencement Address?*"

"It is widely considered a farce," she said. "A forgery

written by white supremacist nut jobs and academically discredited." She paused. "Funny, though..."

"What is?"

"No one's pulled that file in my memory."

"So?" I said.

"You're the *second* person to get it off the shelf this week."

CHAPTER 7

ime for the symposium.

It's funny how academic things go on on the Notre Dame campus every football weekend. They are all over the place, in a wide variety of topics and themes, usually with something ND is famous for-religion, law, ethics, engineering, you name it. Then there's the self-serving authors crowding into the bookstore library hawking their latest.

I didn't know what was harder to process - that we were still holding the symposium after two murders, or that I was supposed to talk about antisocial behavior while the entire ND community was reeling. It wasn't the kind of thing the faithful expected to face. Big football weekends brought intensity, sure - even hostility - but it was all supposed to stay in the make-believe world of sports.

Still, the symposium involved federal grants, donors, and scholars, so it wasn't something easily canceled. The university hadn't yet issued any statement about the murders, or what they meant for the game and the weekend. I assumed a message was being drafted somewhere - one that guaranteed the "safety of everyone on campus." I wasn't sure that would be accurate.

The truth was, I didn't know what the hell was going on. Nobody did. It wasn't an overstatement to say a madman was on the loose - even if that sounded melodramatic.

There were empty seats in the conference room on the third floor of O'Shag. Faculty showed up out of duty, students out of habit, and a few reporters lingered outside hoping for a soundbite. The whole thing had a weird vibe.

Brian served as moderator, something I'd seen him do many times over the years. He had the perfect temperament for it - intellectual, ego in check, and socially adept enough to handle the inevitable long-winded professor who had to be politely cut off.

I took my seat at the panel table. Reverend Lacey sat next to me, jaw tight, flipping through a stack of note cards. Brian caught my eye and gave a weary shrug. To his right sat an attractive, sharp-looking woman who immediately drew my attention - and curiosity. Next to her was a middle-aged man who wasn't wearing a collar but had that unmistakable priestly air. You spend decades in Catholic institutions, and you develop a kind of clerical radar.

Hartman welcomed everyone in his usual steady tone. "In light of recent tragic events, we shall proceed - and in faith, we hope and pray the campus remains peaceful this weekend."

It felt forced and perfunctory, but this was Notre Dame. It had to be said.

Father Lacey went first. His topic: *"The Theology of Redemptive Suffering."*

He was polished in that academic way that would seem pompous and exhausting anywhere else. He bellowed more than he spoke, his tone carrying an air of authority meant to signal that this was *the* way to view the subject - his way.

"One of the great tragedies of modern moral discourse is our refusal to accept that history unfolds in seasons. We insist on applying the language of peace to moments that were defined by war, and then wonder why our judgments feel hollow."

Then he paused for full effect.

"I am reminded of Ecclesiastes 3:1-8."

> For everything there is a season,
> and a time for every matter under heaven...
> a time to break down, and a time to build up...
> a time for war, and a time for peace."

Somewhere David Crosby was spinning.

He kept on.

"When men take judgment into their own hands, even for causes they believe righteous, they often confuse devastation with justice. Scripture warns us what happens when vengeance is mistaken for moral clarity."

Pause. Ugh.

"Romans 12:19 - "Vengeance Is Mine.""

> Beloved, never avenge yourselves,
> but leave room for the wrath of God.

Now, I know my knowledge of scripture leaves a lot to be desired, but other than the pretentious bombast, I had no idea what the fuck this guy was talking about.

I struggled to focus. Instead, I kept rehearsing what I would say when it was my turn. Not very collegial, I know, but after years of these symposia, my mind tended to glaze over the performances.

A few heads in the audience nodded. Others stared blankly. One man near the back - broad-shouldered, wearing a Georgia Bulldogs windbreaker - leaned forward, elbows on knees, eyes locked on the podium.

My turn came next. *"The Psychology and Theology of Ritualized Violence."*

I stuck to the script. "When acts of violence adopt a religious form, they stop being random. They become messages - to the self, to a group, to history. The danger is when the perpetrator stops seeing himself as a killer and starts believing he's a prophet."

I had worked hard on that line and thought it was gold. The crowd did not break into applause. I told myself they were simply exercising the academic restraint the setting demanded.

Brian then introduced the woman to his right. She had sharp features, wore a smart, slim-fitting navy suit, and exuded confidence.

"Our next panelist joins us from somewhat warmer climates - and from a distinguished academic background that bridges history, theology, and cultural studies," Brian said. "Dr. Claire Bennett is an Associate Professor of Religious History at the University of Georgia, where her research focuses on Civil War-era Southern religious movements, particularly how theological narratives shaped - and continue to shape - cultural identity and conflict in the American South.

"Her work has appeared in *The Journal of Southern Religion* and *Church History Quarterly*. She's also the author of *Faith, Fire, and the Lost Cause: Religion and Resistance in the Postbellum South*, which I highly recommend. Please join me in welcoming Dr. Claire Bennett."

University of Georgia. Fitting, given the weekend.

She thanked everyone and began, her soft Southern drawl polished by academia.

"In the decades following the Civil War," she said, "religious narratives in the American South did not simply reflect the trauma of defeat - they actively reshaped it."

"Churches - both Protestant and Catholic - became spaces where the 'Lost Cause' was not only mourned but mythologized. Sermons and sacred language reframed Confederate sacrifice as a holy cause, as martyrdom, as suffering parallel to the Passion itself.

"Particularly pervasive was the use of fire - both literal and metaphorical - as cleansing. From the burning of Atlanta to the destruction of Southern identity, these events were reinterpreted through religious imagery, with General Sherman often cast not just as a military villain but as an anti-Christ figure.

"This spiritualized grievance laid the groundwork for later extremist movements - from twentieth-century white nationalism to modern neo-Confederate ideology - which still invoke theological justifications for racial violence and cultural revenge.

"Understanding those roots," she concluded, "is essential

if we're to understand the persistence - and the danger - of such narratives today."

She was sharp, no question. It didn't hurt that she was sharp-looking with an athletic build under her smart business suit.

During the Q&A, the first few questions were the usual academic fluff. Then a hand went up from a gray-haired guy in the back.

"Isn't it dangerous," he said, "to ascribe modern motives to ancient honor? The Confederacy fought for many things, including states' rights, freedom, and independence."

Brian leaned forward, but I cut in first.

"It's dangerous," I said, "when honor gets distorted into grievance. That's when you get martyrs - and those who want to make them."

The man continued.

"Yet, dominance, destruction, and deconstruction were justified by the Union?"

Lacey chimed in. I think he even added some more bass to his voice...if that was possible.

"We like to pretend history is something we can simply apologize for and move beyond. Scripture is far less optimistic. It recognizes that moral consequence travels across generations, whether we acknowledge it or not. Exodus 20:5 -

Visiting the iniquity of the fathers upon the children to the third and fourth generation.

Huh?

Thankfully, time was running out. Brian did the closing, somehow summing up the disjoint opinions as if some consensus had been reached.

Hey, I got tickets to the game for it, so it was all worthwhile. I was glad to duck out. The air in O'Shag felt stale.

Before I could process the dynamics of the symposium, my phone buzzed again.

Link had texted:

Another body. Get to the Lakes. Now.

CHAPTER 8

I love the campus. I love exploring it whenever I get back-but not like this, and not under these circumstances. Things didn't feel real, and I felt a different kind of anxiety than I was used to. It had something to do with the juxtaposition of this place I loved, a place that was so much a part of my past, and the fact that, in a sense, it was being defiled.

I passed some ND fans who were hooting and hollering with Big Mac. Alcohol was already involved, and the silliness appropriate to the game was out of place with the other events. Big Earl was just a few hundred feet up the quad, and he was shouting something about the South rising again, which added to my uneasiness. I could hear the Vikings in the distance chanting their nonsensical rants, and all of it was getting under my skin. Usually, it all made me laugh.

Last year's incident-the shootout with the bad guys, the kidnapping of my little sister and Rocky-might have made me a hero, but it also made me a wounded man. I flinched more. I worried more. I slept less. There were nights when the nightmares brought it all back. The hero bullshit didn't do much for me when all that lay in the background.

Still, Link was my best friend, and now we were in this together.

What had become the usual crowd had gathered at a remote spot around St. Joe Lake. It was far from any buildings, in an area where the path was shielded by high bushes and marshes growing along the lake's edge. A deep tension tightened in my gut and began to spread through me. It went beyond uneasiness-I felt dizzy and a little sick to my stomach.

As I approached, I could hear Link-but it was different this time.

His voice was raised, sharp with that angry edge I knew too well-the one he got when he'd had enough.

"Don't you fuckin' pull rank on me, asshole. I don't care who the fuck you work for."

Link had taken a step toward a burly guy in an FBI golf shirt and sunglasses. He had one of those fit-cop builds, and the shirt was just a little too tight-probably by design.

Jo stood expressionless, nonplussed but keeping her distance.

"Back up, chief," the agent said. "You better settle down."

"Don't fuckin' tell me to settle down. Don't forget-this is my campus, not yours."

The FBI guy sighed, patronizingly, taking a barely noticeable step back. It was a bad scene for Link. Over the years, I'd learned the signs of when he was getting close to losing it. In college, it meant bar fights, school suspension, and a broken nose. Right now, the stakes were a lot higher.

It was time to intervene-to save my friend from the world of trouble he was about to walk into.

"Link!" I shouted, loud enough to startle the circle of men and interrupt the confrontation. "C'mere!"

He walked the fifteen steps toward me, still seething. I could read it in his face. Time to distract him-a skill I'd honed long ago. More than once, it got us back to Alumni Hall instead of the parking lot outside The Commons with a couple of pissed-off townies.

"Who's the victim?" I asked, steering him away from the standoff.

"ND adjunct instructor. Faculty member of the Catholic Social Justice Colloquium." Link paused, knowing my next question. "They look at things like social injustice and racism within Catholic teaching."

"Shit, you're kidding me. This isn't random at all," I said. "Any more symbolism?"

"Yeah. Another burnt piece of Sherman's address. And this." He showed me a photo on his phone. "The FBI took the actual evidence. That's what that pleasant exchange was about."

I read it aloud:

"Scourging at the Pillar: The weight of betrayal. The Northern church kneels to power, not to God. Cleanse the altars. Fire shall precede justice."

"Another of the Sorrowful Mysteries." it was Jo. She just appeared.

"The Northern church-what the hell does that even mean?" I asked, mostly to myself.

"You got me," Link said.

"You want to take a walk?" I thought it would be good

to get Link away. "I did some library research yesterday. I'm an egghead-it's what I do. But this might be important."

Link looked over his shoulder. "They ordered me to stop looking into things. I don't intend to listen, but there's no harm in letting them think I'm following orders. Let's take a walk."

We headed around the perimeter of the lake. A light rain had started to fall.

"Jo, I'll see you back at the station." Link shouted. She nodded and headed out.

"Sherman marched on Georgia and burned it down," I said. "All of it-everything in his path. Then he stayed and burned houses and plantations mostly for the hell of it. Atlanta had already surrendered. He didn't have to do it. He was stepping on the throat of the Confederacy."

"Am I supposed to feel bad? This was about slavery. Not that many generations ago. My own great-great-great-grandfather."

"Yeah, don't know much about it. It's kind of weird in my family. My grandfather didn't want to know about any of it. My dad did some lineage stuff but doesn't talk about it."

"No doubt Sherman won the war. But it was also about something more-about exercising superiority. About breaking the spirit of the Confederacy."

"If I remember right, the Confederates were awful to the Union's prisoners of war, weren't they?"

"Yeah. And that fueled Sherman and his men. Still, the South has never forgotten what he did."

"It was a few years ago, Trace."

I smirked. "I went to the library and read Sherman's

address. Mostly about right and wrong and bringing the country back together. But there's also a *second draft*-one that revels in the burning and destruction of the South. It taunts the Confederacy. That's the one the white supremacists-the Lost Cause crowd-latch onto."

"What exactly is the 'Lost Cause'? The loss of the right to enslave people?"

"No. It's the idea that instead of remembering the South's defeat as the consequence of defending slavery, the Lost Cause reframed the Confederacy as a noble, heroic struggle for states' rights, honor, and tradition-one tragically lost to overwhelming Northern aggression and industrial might."

"That's a hell of a generalization."

"Yeah. For sure."

"Did Sherman actually write two commencement speeches? That doesn't make sense."

"The experts say no. But the fringe supremacists insist he did. To them, it's proof of injustice. Sherman is seen as Satan in the South. It's all over message boards and in KKK-adjacent groups."

"What does that have to do with ND?"

"Sherman's son went here. His daughter went to Saint Mary's. His wife lived on campus during the war. They were close with Father Sorin."

"Okay, okay, slow down. This may all be true, but who's doing this? A crazed, white-supremacist Georgia fan who knows the ins and outs of our campus, our history-and somehow thinks he's getting revenge?"

We had made our way from the lake to the north side of campus, near the ND fire department.

"Link, it points to something like that. What else could it be?"

"That's just great," he said. "So what do we do next? Eighty thousand people are descending on this campus in the next twenty-four hours. This is all fascinating, but the administration isn't thrilled about the publicity."

"I think we need to find out more about white supremacists-and how they connect to the University of Georgia, General Sherman, and Notre Dame," I said.

"Sure. That'll be easy. Bodies piling up, cryptic messages, and the country's biggest sports weekend." He shook his head. "Just another day in paradise."

"I know where I can start."

"Oh yeah?"

"My new best friend-Dr. Claire Bennett, from the symposium. University of Georgia. History professor. Probably staying at the Morris Inn."

"Have at it," Link said. "Go Irish."

CHAPTER 9

I called the front desk at the Morris Inn and had them ring Dr. Bennett's room, but there was no answer. It was late afternoon, and the misty rain had returned, though it was light and felt good on the walk back. Friday night on the eve of the biggest game of the year meant the hotel lobby would be jammed. It was all part of it. I headed in, hoping I'd find her in the crowded mess.

Once through the sliding glass doors, I was hit with the din of excited conversation and mini-reunions. All ages were there-from the ones who graduated last year to current students drinking with mom and dad, to old-timers. I spotted Terry Hanratty standing in a circle, laughing with kicker Bob Thomas and All-American tight end turned oral surgeon Ken MacAfee. They had that look of old jocks who knew their place and enjoyed it.

Digger Phelps's voice could be heard, and I saw him slap the back of Dick Vitale while John Paxson looked on, amused. Alumni watched like mere mortals, rubbing shoulders with heroes they shared a lineage with.

Then I spotted her-reading from an iPad on the velvet couch by the lobby library. She shared the couch with two heavyset, seventy-something alums in navy blue quarter-zips, sipping highballs. She didn't look up when I approached.

"Go Dawgs. Sic 'em, sic 'em, sic 'em," I said, standing over her.

She looked up hopefully, then frowned.

"Oh-Dr. Curran. I thought for a second I'd found a friend."

"Well, maybe you have. Can I join you for a drink?"

She seemed to consider it.

"You know, this may be hard to believe, but this place gets on my nerves just a tad. Suppose you get a drink and then you could tour me around this blessed place?"

Just a hint of sarcasm.

"Deal. But it's going to take a second to get a drink. I hope Murph's on."

Murph had been a bartender at the Morris Inn since the '60s. We got to know each other when I worked as a busboy there for a couple of years. He'd hook me up.

"Murph!" I shouted. He turned slightly. He was swamped, but in a second, I had a full rocks glass of bourbon in my hand. He didn't have time to chat but gave me an old friend's wink.

When I got back to the couch, she was standing. She was wearing snug stretch jeans, red Hokas, and an untucked white dress T-shirt. She slung a light blue silk baseball-style jacket over her shoulder.

"Go Irish," she said, rolling her eyes.

The cool, misty air felt refreshing after the stuffy, crowded lobby.

"Oh my God, that feels better," she said as we hit Notre Dame Avenue.

"Yeah, the air feels nice."

"That too," she said with a smirk.

"Had a bit too much of *shaking down the thunder*?" I said.

"I suppose they're no worse than Dawg Nation."

We walked onto the campus proper. Of course, Alumni Hall-the center of the universe-was there to greet us. Hanging from the third floor in the quad where Link and I lived was a banner that read:

How do you get a UGA grad off your porch? Pay for the pizza!

"This is where I lived as an undergrad." I nodded toward Alumni.

"Clever banner. What is it about Notre Dame that makes y'all feel superior?" The "y'all" was subtle but charming as hell.

"Y'all?" I said, smiling.

She gave me a mock-threatening look.

"We do tend to be that way-a little."

"Oh, *a little?*" she said.

We took a left along the South Quad sidewalk. The moon hung full over Rockne Memorial in the distance.

"Did you know our School of Public and International Affairs consistently ranks in the top five nationally? The MPA program is one of the best in the country-not just the South. We're also a national leader in cognitive and behavioral science. The Institute of Neuroscience has received major NIH grants for work on neuroplasticity and aging. Deliver *that* with your fucking pizza," she said.

There was something about her cursing that made her even more likable.

"Touche," I said. "Too bad you're getting your asses kicked tomorrow."

"Oh, please."

We passed Dillon Hall, then the South Dining Hall, and went by the construction for the new dormitories. Fisher and Pangborn had been razed for modern replacements-more comfortable than the old cinder-block heat traps built to house Navy officers during WWII, an arrangement that had saved the university from bankruptcy.

We turned right in front of the Rock.

"What do you know about white supremacy, Sherman, the Civil War, and Notre Dame?" I knew the transition was abrupt.

"Hmm. I guess small talk's over," she sighed. "Look, slavery and all that came with it is indefensible. The Lost Cause rationalization-that it was about 'states' rights' instead of slavery-is also indefensible nonsense. That said, the burning of Atlanta, South Carolina, and everything in Sherman's path after the war was already won isn't exactly a proud chapter, either."

"War, right?"

"In today's world, it would be called a war crime-not far from terrorism. Sherman burned civilian homes and plantations, even those with no history of slavery. He torched homes of Northerners and Union sympathizers, too."

"He did institute Special Field Orders No. 15."

"Forty acres and a mule for freed slaves? Don't get me started. They never got it. It was a ploy to keep the freedmen on the Union side." Her voice had a touch of urgency-and annoyance. "I won't rationalize anything, but context matters. By the way, when did Notre Dame start admitting Black students?"

"There was a Navy officer in '44."

"Part of the Navy program. When did *actual* students start?"

"The fifties, I guess."

"So you were a decade ahead of Georgia."

"Father Sorin housed some emancipated slaves and was vocal against the war."

She gave me a look.

"Like, 'some of my best friends are Black.'"

"Okay, okay - point made." I didn't want to go down that rabbit hole. We went down the steps beside the Rock and hit the path around St. Mary's Lake. The candles at the Grotto glowed in the distance. "Tell me about fringe supremacists - what this could have to do with what's happening here."

"No doubt, Sherman's march still evokes hatred - and probably should. He gives extremists something to rally around. The war was broad, but his march wasn't. It's a clear, concentrated symbol of what the Union did to the Confederacy."

"You know he gave the commencement address here just months after the surrender."

"Of course. And his son went here before his early death."

"You know about the alternative commencement speech?"

"The one the victims had on them? Of course. It isn't real, but it's become a rallying point for extremists."

"And Notre Dame itself?"

"Well, add that history - plus the role football plays in our culture - and it's not hard to imagine a deranged person coming here to make a point."

"You know anyone like that?"

"I don't have a white hood in the closet."

"I mean, do you know anyone from Georgia who might?"

"I know a professor who studies such things."

"Could I give them a call?"

"Sure. I'll give you the number."

We were halfway around the lake and found ourselves in front of the Grotto. The mist had turned into a light rain. Above the glow of the candles, the Golden Dome shone through a soft fog.

"This place is beautiful," Claire said, looking up. "No doubt - very special."

CHAPTER 10

The quiet beauty of the candlelit Grotto and the mist-golden glow of the Dome was interrupted. "Unga munga sanna ranna foost! Unga munga sanna ranna foost!" came the command, followed by a loud bass drum and out-of-tune trumpets assaulting the ears.

"What the hell?" Claire said.

"Oh, you're in for a treat. The Viking Parade." We walked up the road on the side of the Grotto and past the crypt at the back of the Basilica. And there they were, about 25 strong. Grown men reliving their adolescent days of idiocy. They were marching away from the Dome and heading toward the South Quad, undoubtedly for a tour.

"Unga munga sanna ranna foost! Unga munga sanna ranna foost!" the leader shouted. I wondered if the toothless guy ever mixed it up.

Big Earl, the crazed UGA fan, fell in with them at the back. Lunacy makes strange bedfellows.

"The South will rise tomorrow!" he bellowed in between Viking chants. The Vikings were oblivious.

"You know the class and dignity of Notre Dame really shines, doesn't it?" Claire said.

"Uh-huh. The Zahm guys were all class. I see they've adopted your man Earl."

"A couple of fine examples of our institutions."

"You want to follow them back to the hotel?" I said, trying to disguise any hint of hope or desperation.

"Um, I don't think I'm ready to head back in there. I'm going to do some walking and thinking. I like walking in new places."

"Sure, enjoy." There was part of me that wished I was invited to go along, but I let that go and went back to The Morris Inn. Claire was formidable. She was strong but didn't seem to be driven by ego. She was opinionated, but she owned it, and she seemed to care about understanding different perspectives. I was already back to Clashmore Mike, walking in the rain and realizing how much cognitive energy I was spending on Claire. It wasn't lost on me how physically attractive she was, and despite her allegiance to ND's football enemy, the combination of her slight lilting drawl and her intelligence really piqued my interest.

At the corner of Alumni Hall I saw a figure that vaguely looked familiar. It was Jo. She had a knapsack almost as big as her strapped to her back.

"Hey Jo!" I called to her.

She stopped.

"Hello Doctor Curran."

"Where you going this late on the night before a game?"

"The Library. It is open for another hour and I need something."

"Going to the game?"

She frowned. If you could measure disdain it would be in the 90th percentile.

"No."

"Oh, yeah, not your thing," I said. "Well, Go Irish!"

She frowned and exhaled and headed to the library.

I still had a way with the co-eds.

I didn't try to figure it out. Instead, I just headed inside the still jam-packed lobby and went right over to see Murph for some reinforcements. He showed no sign of fatigue; he was carrying the same level of energy that he had hours ago. Our eyes met, he winked, and before long, I had another substantial Knob Creek in my hand.

"Come by when we can catch up," he said while making a martini with cocktail onions, not olives.

"Curran! You asshole!" I heard a somewhat familiar voice. I whirled around.

"Oh, fuck you, Flanagan!" It was Terry Flanagan, another Alumni Dawg who lived across the hall from me during my junior and senior years. In a moment, he was joined by Mike Murray and Jake Sebastian, two of his three roommates in his quad.

"Where's Burnsie?" Dennis Burns was the fourth quad roommate.

"Burns is a pussy. He never comes back. Got a master's at Northwestern and turned on us," Murray said.

"Might have something to do with putting the Icy Hot in his shorts or farting into his pillow," I said, remembering some of the, literally, sophomoric pranks Burns always seemed to be the target of.

"There's that," Jake said.

"Hey, what the hell do you make of the killer lost on campus?" Flanagan said.

"You've heard? Yeah, talk about a loss of innocence," I said.

"I don't remember all that much innocence when we were here. Immaturity, obnoxiousness, but not innocence," Jake said, though "innocence" kind of came out "innoshense."

"I heard some shit about General Sherman-I never heard about his ND connection until last night," Flanagan said. I began to realize information was starting to leak out into the masses.

"Yeah, it is like trying to fight the Civil War all over again," Murray said.

That knocked me back. Like trying to fight the Civil War all over again... That's exactly what it was.

The phone vibrated with a text. It was Link. "You need to see this. Don't tell anyone you're coming. Just get here." Attached was a grainy photo of a statue. It looked like Father Sorin, but someone had draped it in a Confederate flag. A small wooden cross had been planted at the base, with the words "The Face of the Enemy."

The bourbon buzz I'd been nursing all night disappeared in a flash, replaced by a rush of adrenaline. I made a quick, probably borderline rude goodbye and didn't tell anyone where I was going. Link's instructions were clear.

The mist had turned into a steady rain, making the campus darker and, with everything that was happening, far more ominous. The campus still buzzed with this year's *game of the century* craziness-stereos blared, shouts echoed through the night, and the usual din of college partying filled the air. But underneath it all, I felt a sense of urgency that matched whatever was waiting for me.

I cut across the God Quad, the Dome barely visible behind sheets of rain and fog. The night didn't need anything else to make it creepier, but this did. I felt it in my bones-a mix of anxiety, dread, and the echo of another time when everything had gone wrong. The difference was that this was Notre Dame-my place of hope and dreams, the halcyon corner of my past. At least it used to be.

A flash of light reflected off the statue of Father Sorin. When I followed it, I saw it was coming from Link's flashlight. I came up on him quietly; he didn't notice at first; his focus was absolute-the kind of focus you get when your whole life has been about solving the puzzle of human ugliness.

"It's still there," he said in a low voice. "No one's noticed. Not yet. I didn't report it. Figured you'd want to see it first."

We stood about ten feet from the Sorin statue. From a distance, it might've looked like a prank-one of those weird game-day traditions where someone hangs underwear on a statue or dresses it in a team jersey. But up close, it was something else entirely.

Someone had draped a Confederate flag over Sorin's shoulders like a cloak. Beneath it, at the base, next to the cross, a rosary was spread out to be seen.

The Sorrowful Mysteries: More to Come

"Jesus," I muttered.

Link crossed his arms. "That's not some Georgia sophomore getting overexcited about tomorrow. Someone's interpreting the Sorrowful Mysteries."

"Yeah," I said, my mind racing. "But it's more than that. They're rewriting them-twisting them. Making the Church complicit, or maybe the North. Sorin as 'the face of the enemy'? That's insane. Sorin was anti-slavery. He housed freed slaves on campus."

"To the guy doing this shit? It doesn't matter. Sorin's Union. Sorin's Northern. Sorin's Notre Dame."

"And Sherman."

We stood in silence for a moment, the rain soaking us both.

"I don't think this guy's just acting out some sick fantasy," Link said. "He's staging something. Building a narrative."

"We need to warn people," I said.

"Warn who? The FBI? They already think I'm a nuisance. You too."

"Then we keep going. You and me. We'll figure this out."

Link nodded. "You still got that photo from the last one-the one with the line about betrayal?"

I pulled out my phone and brought it up.

"The Northern Church kneels to power, not to God," Link read aloud. "So now we've got betrayal, the Northern Church, Sorin as enemy..."

"And Sherman as the demon."

Link looked at the flag again. "This guy's got an obsession. He's not just some psycho. He's educated. He knows his history."

"And his symbolism."

I took a few more pictures, then carefully peeled the Confederate flag off Sorin's shoulders and folded it.

"Evidence?" Link asked.

"No. I think Father Sorin would like me to remove this from his shoulders."

"Hell yeah," Link said.

We started walking back toward the inn, both of us quiet. The fog was thick now, swallowing the paths and muffling sound. The Grotto glowed dimly in the distance.

"Hey," I said. "What if he's not just staging murders? What if this ends with something big?"

Link stopped walking. "What are you thinking?"

"Notre Dame Stadium. Tomorrow. Eighty thousand people. What better place to make your point about Northern betrayal-about the so-called desecration of the South, about Sherman, Sorin, the whole damn narrative?"

He exhaled slowly. "Jesus."

We resumed walking.

"I'll talk to Claire again in the morning. Maybe her contact down at Georgia has something."

"You trust her?"

"I don't know. I like her. She's smart. She's... complicated."

Link smirked. "That's code for you're in trouble."

"Maybe. But I'm not stupid."

He nodded. "Good. Don't be."

When I finally got back to my room, I peeled off my wet clothes, poured a bourbon, and sat in the armchair by the window. Campus stretched before me in shadows and lamplight. I sipped slowly, going over it all again.

The Sorrowful Mysteries. Sherman. The Lost Cause. White supremacy dressed up in the robes of martyrdom.

Something was coming. I could feel it in my chest.

CHAPTER 11

The image of the Confederate flag on Father Sorin might have looked like a tailgating prank by a few UGA freshmen, but when you knew the backstory unfolding, it was far more ominous and unnerving. Those bastards were sending a sick message, and whatever it was they were trying to pull off just couldn't be allowed.

Of course, stopping something when you didn't even know what it was wasn't the easiest trick in the book.

The overcast gray sky bled through the blinds as I sipped coffee from the cheap in-room machine - after two failed attempts to figure out how it worked. I wiped the spilled coffee off the dresser with one of the Morris Inn towels.

This wasn't the first time the campus had been under siege.

The Ku Klux Klan, headquartered right here in Indiana, had decided in the 1920s that they didn't like the progress this Catholic university was making. They planned to march on campus. Father Cavanaugh, then president, forbade the students to leave and told them to ignore the situation.

That's not what they did.

Instead, thousands of students went to the train station and met the Klansmen as they tried to get off. There's no other way to say it - the students rioted, attacking the KKK thugs and forcing them back onto the train. Then they marched to Klan headquarters in South Bend. Next door was a market, and the students grabbed that most fitting Irish Catholic weaponsweapon - potatoes - and stoned the building.

The story goes that quarterback Harry Stuhldreher was summoned to reach the red-lit cross on top of the headquarters. He did, and with the same arm that threw touchdowns, he shattered every light in the crucifix.

Makes me prouder than any bowl win.

The Klan was something different than what was in front of us today. The Klan was an out-front public showing. This - this was an insidious and evil riddle, teasing horrific consequences in a time when our country was ripe for rationalizing lunacy.

Father Sorin, depicted as the face of the enemy, cloaked in a Confederate flagflag, sickened my stomach. The killer wasn't just reenacting the Sorrowful Mysteries - he was rewriting them, repurposing Catholic symbolism as Confederate martyrdom. This was more than theater. It was an ideology. It was propaganda.

I texted Link: *Anything?No response.*

It was still game day. The campus murders had become a subtext to the weekend - something whispered about, not acknowledged. There was no public talk of symbolism or a larger threat. No, this was just a bad coincidence on a busy campus. The game was too big, too important. This was college football - and it wasn't taken lightly by the Notre Dame faithful, the students, the subway alumni, or the TV networks, sponsors, and all the others who profited from the spectacle.

This wasn't a D3 game between Plattsburgh and Potsdam State that drew 300 fans. This was Notre Dame vs. Georgia - with over 80,000 in attendance and millions watching on TV.

Despite all that, what was happening couldn't be trivialized.

It wasn't even 7 a.m., but I dressed, grabbed my jacket, and headed out. A few tailgaters were already up, setting up tents and grills like it was any other game day. There was something unnerving about it - all that festivity, while someone out there was turning the campus into a twisted shrine.

Claire agreed to meet me for breakfast at Rohr's, the Morris Inn's casual dining room. She was already seated in a corner booth, hair pulled back, wearing a navy turtleneck and glasses. She looked more like a professor than a football fan.

"Sleep?" I asked, sliding into the seat across from her.

"Not"Not much," she said. "You?"

"None."None."

The waiter came by and took our order. I just wanted decent coffee and a muffin big enough to quiet the hunger so I could think.

"I reached out to a colleague," Claire said, pulling out her phone. "Dr. Sorrell. She teaches American religious movements at Georgia. Her recent focus has been on

Christian Identity and post-Civil War Confederate theology."

"Confederate theology?"

"It's a thing. A very scary thing. She says there's been a resurgence over the last decade - forums, manifestos, YouTube sermons. A whole subculture romanticizing the South as a holy land betrayed by the Union - and by Catholics, in particular."

"Why Catholics?"

"Because they were abolitionists. Because they were immigrants. Because Notre Dame was Union."

I nodded, remembering the flag draped over Sorin's bronze shoulders.

"She sent me something," Claire said, handing over her phone. "An excerpt from a fringe blog. They interpret Sherman's March as the 'Northern Purge,' and they call Sorin a *Vatican Agent of Subjugation.* Did that phrase appear in any of your killer's messages?"

I frowned. "Not yet. But it fits."

Claire leaned forward. "This isn't just about history, Trace, it's theology. Twisted, theology sure, but deeply rooted. He thinks he's on a mission."

"Who's the author?"

"Jeffrey Davis, just like the president. Disgraced professor at UGA. Brilliant, stolid, the kind of intellectual that talks in triads but a violent racist, Lost Cause champion. He taught in that program."

I pushed my plate away. "Then what's the finale? What's his crucifixion?"

Claire didn't answer right away.

"Notre Dame Stadium," I said. "It has to be."

"He wouldn't get far with a weapon," she said.

"No."No. But a message? A symbol? A spectacle?"

The pieces were moving, but I didn't know how they fit.

My phone buzzed. Link.

Come to the library basement. You need to see this.

I looked at Claire. "You want to come?"

She nodded. "Let's go."

We left through the east door. The campus was waking up, and the sounds of drums and marching band practice echoed through the cold morning air. It felt like we were running out of time.

CHAPTER 12

The first floor of the Hesburgh Library housed the archives section, and it had that musty scent of forgotten things. Old maps, archival boxes, and metal cabinets lined the narrow hallway leading to the staff-only area. Link was waiting at the end with Jo, clipboard under one arm, reading glasses slipping down his nose.

"You found something?" I asked, still catching my breath from the cold air outside and the walk from the hotel.

Link nodded and led us into a back room. "Jo cross-referenced some language from the Sorin scene with old campus publications using AI. She looked at fringe student newsletters, op-eds, and campus police reports. She got a hit. This came up."

He dropped a folder on the table. Inside were photocopies from a 2003 disciplinary hearing. The name at the top made my stomach turn.

"Russell Blake," I said.

Claire leaned in. "You know him?"

"He lived in Dillon. He was a freshman when I was a

junior. Weird dude. He ran an alt-right student blog before that even had a name. CampusThe campus tried to ignore him until he staged that stunt on the South Quad."

"Stunt?" Claire said.

"A memorial to the fallen Confederacy. He wore a white robe without a hood - but everyone got the idea," I said.

"I remember that," Link said. "Didn't he get expelled?"

"Yeah. After they found racist flyers in several dorms and one slipped under a Black student's door with a noose drawn on it. They never proved it was Blake, but everyone knew. The rumor was he went back down south and disappeared. Literally. Not even on social media."

Claire's voice tightened. "You think he's back?"

Link nodded. "It's more than that. Look at the pseudonym on this blog Dr. Sorrell flagged."

He pointed to a screen: **VeritasRex1837.**After the signaturesignature, there was in italics "*All that is necessary for the triumph of evil is for good men to do nothing.*" *Jeff Davis*

"Notre Dame's founding year," Claire said. "And a Confederacy reference and maybe a tribute to Davis, the disgraced prof."

"Latin for 'truth is king,'" I added. "That was Blake's whole brand back then. And a quote from Davis?"

"Yeah, except Davis never said it. Another Lost Cause bullshit attribution." Claire shook her head.

"He's staging a revisionist history," Link said. "A personal vendetta dressed up as Southern martyrdom."

My pulse kicked up. "If it's Blake, he knows this place. He knows the game-day schedule, the security gaps, the tunnels,tunnels; hell, he could still have access cards."

Claire turned pale. "And if he's running through The Sorrowful MysteriesMysteries, he's almost done."

"Holy shit," I said, sinking into one of the burgundy leather chairs. The file felt heavier than it should've in my hands. "What else do we know?"

Link rubbed his jaw. "Nothing current. No driver's license, no traceable income, no voter registration. But Dr. Sorrell forwarded a PDF of an underground zine from a Southern identity group. One article was signed - *R.B., Dillon Exile.* That was two months ago. Maybe he enrolled at Georgia. Is it hard to enroll in college under a fake name?"

"For the guy pulling this shit off? Piece of cake." Claire's brow furrowed. "So, he's broadcasting. Cryptically, but he wants this seen."

"And decoded," I added. "That's what the Sorrowful Mysteries are - a message built for someone like me to read."

"You mean Catholics?" Claire asked.

"No," I said. "Notre Dame men."

That landed hard.

Claire folded her arms. "So what's next? What's What's the next mystery?"

I tried to recall the traditional order. "*The Carrying of the Cross.* A moment of weakness... maybe shame or humiliation. What would that be here?"

Claire spoke slowly. "Blake believed the University betrayed white Southern values. Maybe the scene will reflect that."

Link flipped through a few more pages. "There's a lot of

fire-and-brimstone stuff in this writing. Judgment, cleansing, purification."

"Claire, is it possible the killer sees himself as an avenger?" I asked. "A kind of Confederate Christ figure, sacrificing himself to make a point?"

She hesitated, then nodded. "More like a saint of vengeance. These movements don't always follow theology - they repurpose it. He's mixing martyrdom with crusade. That makes him unpredictable."

"And very dangerous."

Link's phone buzzed. He checked it, then went pale. "Campus PD. Another scene."

"Where?" I asked.

"Zahm. Or what's left of it."

Claire frowned. "Didn't that dorm close?"

"Exactly," I said, already on my feet. "That's why it's perfect. It's used to house students whose current dorms are in transition."

CHAPTER 13

Claire and I made it over to Zahm in less than ten minutes. Technically, it was no longer Zahm-it was housing the guys from Morrissey while their old dorm got fixed up. Morrissey was one of the cooler halls on campus, and I'd always liked the guys from there. They called it "Morrissey Manor." It was old and had some unique rooms and spaces.

Link and Jo was in the rector's office with Father Billings, the priest in charge of the dorm, and the RA from the first floor, Josh Fonseca. They were mid-conversation when we entered. Father Billings looked genuinely concerned.

"I have no idea what it means, but it looks really sinister," the priest said. "It isn't funny like a game-day prank."

Father wasn't wearing a collar. He was in his forties and dressed in jeans, a blue button-down Oxford shirt, and Nikes. With his sandy brown hair and easy demeanor, he looked more like a grad student than clergy.

"Hey, Father, I'm Trace Curran. I'm in for a symposium. This is Claire Bennett from UGA-she's also here for the symposium."

"Which symposium?" he asked.

"The one on psychology, theology, and violence," I said. "I'm a psychologist and work part-time with the CIA. Claire's a PhD in Southern theology."

"Well, Link, looks like you brought the right friends."

Link smiled, but his tone stayed all business.

"Father, okay if we head down into the tunnels?"

"Of course. Here's the key. You can go by yourselves-I don't need to see it again."

The tunnel entrance was in the basement. There was a community room with a big-screen TV, a pool table, and a station for video games. Next to it was the small dorm food shop where you could get bad pizza at night, chips, and other unhealthy snacks.

Off to the right was a door that led to the trash and laundry chutes. ND was one of the only colleges that still did student laundry-though they had a habit of shrinking your Levi's four sizes.

Next to the chutes was a steel door with a deadbolt lock. We had the key, so that gave us passage, but there the legendary stories about students breaking into the tunnels were rampant. Borrowed keys, jimmied locks, or ancient broken doors probably explained it. The grates in front of the South Dining Hall were a favorite entrance.

Inside, the tunnels had rounded ceilings with dim forty-watt bulbs and were no wider than five feet. It was warm and damp-probably because the tunnels' main function was to carry steam to heat the buildings. It was dark and creepy.

Twenty feet down the passage was a makeshift room divider. A chill went through me as we approached it.

Link took the lead. He had a bright cop flashlight and moved the sheet of plywood that had been crudely nailed up. On the wall was a large Confederate flag. To the left, a sign read: *The South Will Rise Again.* Beneath that, another scrawled message: *Sherman, the Catholics, and Notre Dame's Reckoning is Upon Us!* Both were drawn crudely in Sharpie.

On the table was what looked like an academic paper. Claire picked it up.

"The fake Sherman address," she said, flipping through it.

Link shone the flashlight on a cardboard box beneath the table.

"Check this out. Photos of Father Corby with a red X through his face. Same with Father Sorin. And this woman-same mark."

"Let me see," Claire said. Link handed her the photos.

"Sherman's wife," she said quietly. "In front of St. Mary's Lake." She flipped to the end of the manuscript.

Link pulled out a small antique handgun and a short Confederate sword from the box.

"Jesus. Look at this stuff. What's he trying to tell us?"

I didn't answer.

"Link, what's your last name?" Claire asked suddenly. The question didn't fit the moment. She had closed the manuscript and was staring at Link.

"Uh, I told you when we first met. Christian. Funny time to be getting acquainted."

Claire reopened the manuscript and began to read aloud.

"And to Ben Christian, may he and his heirs-especially his heirs-rot in eternal fire, deserving of their actions."

She looked up at Link.

His face went blank. He took the manuscript from her hands.

"Ben" Christian was my great-great-great-great-grandfather. He was a freed slave. I don't know a whole lot about him."

"You're his heir," I said softly.

We were silent for a long moment.

Then Link's jaw tightened. "This just got personal."

He stared down the tunnel, then back at us. I've seen that type of intensity in his face beforebefore, but it had been a long time.

"I'm going to catch this motherfucker."

CHAPTER 14

We left Zahm and headed toward the Morris Inn. Link's folks were in for the game, and he wanted to give them a quick hello before getting back to the search. Claire wanted to grab a raincoat.

The rain kept falling, mixing with sleet now. The lovely South Bend weather-an acquired taste I never managed to acquire.

Past the God Quad, the campus was filling up fast, and at this pointpoint, it seemed as much red as it did blue, gold, and green. The smell of steak sandwiches wafted from the Knights of Columbus stand. The gargoyles on Alumni Hall jutted out like sentinels keeping watch, and it seemed like Clashmore Mike was shivering in the cold.

That asshole Earl could be heard in the distance. Down by O'Shag, he had a circle of Dawg Nation around him.

"The fire of the South will smite the Irish today! We will rise and get our revenge! Sic 'em! Sic 'em! Sic 'em!"

Ugh.

You could hear The Vikings trying to drown him out with their nonsense chants.

The contrast between the over-the-top game-day insanity and the murders lurking beneath the surface was surreal. The tension had a pulse, and I could feel it under my skin-anxiety without an outlet.

The Morris Inn lobby was jammed with fans escaping the weather. Tim Brown, the Heisman winner, was chatting with Rocket Ismail, and the crowd around them grew by the second. I cracked a smile despite myself. Claire pushed her way through the crowd.

"Come with me outside," she said.

Something in her tone made me follow without a word.

We walked down the driveway to a semi-private spot near the Inn's parking lot. The sleet stung against our faces.

"Blake is dead." Claire's eyes locked on mine, her voice low and intense. "They found him on the Georgia campus. He hung himself from a tree."

"What? When?"

"Five a.m."

I just stared.

"He had a note." She hesitated. "'Sic 'em. Sic 'em. Sic the Catholics today. Make them pay with fire.'"

I thought about it for a moment.

"So"So he left here, flew home, and killed himself. Or, himself? Or was he never here? Why would he kill himself?"

"Because he sensed we were getting close. We had the

history from his time here. The Sorrel connection. He knew he was cornered."

"So it's over?"

Claire shrugged. "Looks that way."

"Just like that? Three dead, a suicide, and we call it done?"

She gave a faint, uneasy smile. "You're the CIA profiler-don't things sometimes end like this when the crazy finally cracks?"

"I mean... maybe. He knew the chase was over. Why wait to face humiliation when you can script your own ending?"

Claire frowned, still thinking. "Do they know on some level that they're insane?"

"Sometimes," I said. "But the delusion always wins."

My phone buzzed. A text from Link.

Blake is dead. The show's over. Be down in a minute.

CHAPTER 15

When Link joined us in the parking lot, he didn't look nearly as relieved as I thought he would.

"Time for a beer and a deep breath?" I said to Link and Claire.

"Yeah, I guess," he said.

"I don't get it-what's up?"

"The Ben Christian thing," he said. "I asked my dad just now, and he got real strange. It was like... I don't know."

Claire looked at me. Her expression said she was comfortable pursuing this with a man she'd known for a day. It was a friend's job. I was the friend.

"What's up?" I asked, trying to keep my tone neutral.

"My dad froze when I told him we found the note. He rubbed the back of his neck like he does when he's stressed. He just said, 'Oh, son.'"

I waited.

"Our grandfather came from a generation when there wasn't really anything like... I don't know, 'Black Pride.' It was a mark of success to assimilate, to be accepted in the white world. My dad was his son."

Claire shot me a glance. She wanted to hear more.

Link continued.

"He said, 'You remember when you were in high school and your mother and I did that ancestry thing?' I sort of did. Then he said, 'We learned about Benjamin.' Shit got pretty intense."

"How so?" I asked.

"Benjamin was a freed slave. He joined the Union Army - Army-something called the 'Colored Regiment,' or some bullshit archaic term like that. They were part of Sherman's March to the Sea."

"Holy shit," I heard myself say.

"That's not all."

I just looked at him, waiting.

"Benjamin Christian was wounded in action. He knew slaves in Georgia. He got a tip about where some Union prisoners of war were being held. He and two other Black soldiers rushed the stockade, took fire, and went up against a dozen Confederate men. They were all wounded, but they took the dozen out. When backup came, they freed the POWs. They were starving, skin and bone, tortured-it was awful."

Link stared into space.

"Holy shit," I said again.

"Sherman found out. He personally thanked the Black soldiers in his quarters. It was after that that he proposed the 'forty acres and a mule' thing. Sherman wasn't exactly a progressive, but he knew bravery when he saw it, and he rewarded them."

Link looked down.

"Why didn't your dad ever tell you?" Claire asked quietly.

Link turned toward her.

"That's the thing. He said he didn't know how. That someday he was going to, but he didn't know where it fit in our lives."

"Amazing story-and a real source of pride for your family," Claire said. "But I think I get your dad's conflict. He came from a line that didn't dwell on such things. They weren't culturally recognized."

"Yeah, I guess. Still a little fucked up." Link let it trail off. "There's something else."

"What's that?" I asked.

"If I didn't know, and my dad didn't know until adulthood... how did Blake know?"

CHAPTER 16

"I mean, the guy was a bug-truly pathological," I said. We were walking toward the stadium, right into the middle of tailgating chaos. The smell of charcoal and bratwurst hung in the air. "There's a good chance he became compulsive about finding stuff out."

"But I didn't even know about Ben. How could he?" Link said.

"Trace is right," Claire said. "For these types, the digging becomes the obsession. The research is the addiction."

"Walk me through it," Link said. "I don't know about Ben. My father knows a little but not even enough to share. His father never talked about it. They were Black soldiers whose service went mostly undocumented. So what kind of research even uncovers that?"

"Wasn't it in Sherman's personal papers?" Claire asked.

"I don't know that. It was in some notes to someone-maybe Blair, Sherman's number two-but it wasn't official documentation. Just personal letters."

"Seems a bit unlikely," Claire said.

"Look, Blake was a nut job," I said. "Crazy enough to hold a Klan-type rally with a white robe on the South Quad. He comes up here for this nonsense, then goes back to Georgia and kills himself. Hard to imagine the guy having limits."

Link wasn't buying it. "I don't know. It just doesn't seem to-"

His phone buzzed, cutting him off.

"Where?" he said. A long pause. "I'll be right there."

Claire and I waited.

Link looked at us, jaw tight. "Another body."

"Where?" I asked.

"On Rockne's grave."

CHAPTER 17

Two of Link's uniforms were standing over the body with Rockne's headstone in the background. Jo was ten feet behind them looking at her phone. It was a modest rectangular headstone, one that seemed undersized for a man of such influence. The cemetery was just to the left of Notre Dame Avenue when you entered campus.

"Captain," the cop on the left greeted Link. He had red hair, fair skin, and clearly worked out. The other cop was a black guy who was built like a middleweight fighter.

The body lay perpendicular across the grave, facedown. It was the body of an older man, probably in his eighties.

"What do we know?" Link asked.

"This was taped to a lamp post by the law school." He handed a note written on lined paper with his gloved hands.

Link read it.

"Go visit the Rock and find out what we think of those that convert. Time for the Carrying of the Cross."

"That's another of the Sorrowful Mysteries," Jo said.

Link looked up at her and then at us.

"Convert?"

"Rockne converted to Catholicism at ND," I said.

"Who is the deceased?" Link always showed respect and didn't use terms like "the body."

"This note says he's Brian Barnes, guard on the '66 championship team," the redhead said, handing Link the second note.

Link read.

"This guard let his man go. Another traitorous convert to be cast into the fire. A failed man of the Confederacy had to pay. Oh, and your team dies today on the field. A symbol on the gridiron...or maybe not. Oh, and how you Ben."

Link paused.

"It finishes with 'How you Ben? LOL.' Ben is spelled B-E-N."

Claire took a small step forward.

"He's threatening the team. He's threatening the game." You could hear the desperation.

Link and I both looked at her.

"But Blake is dead..." I said, almost to myself.

"Someone else all along or someone who took up for him?" Link said.

I looked at Claire.

"Maybe a Blake partner. Maybe an underling carrying out his mission?" she said.

"Mission? What the hell mission is it?"

Jo stepped forward.

"Captain, how does this man get murdered here or transported here on the day of a game and not get noticed?"

Link just looked at everyone like we'd have an explanation.

"Link, we gotta tell the feds," I said. "There's too much at stake."

Link looked at me. He gave me a nod.

CHAPTER 18

The South Bend coroner came for the body. We waited in the cemetery, which made everything that was already weird and uncomfortable even more so. Conversation was getting strained.

"There's an emergency evacuation plan. It was created the year after 9/11. We can shut down the game and get everyone out. Not sure how it would work," Link said.

"Be a lot of unhappy tailgaters," I said.

"Can you imagine trying to round up all those drunken Domers and convince them they were in danger? Herding fuckin' cats." Link shook his head.

"Captain, that plan was completed before the stadium refurbished construction. It is out of date," Jo said.

Claire changed the subject.

"Blake had it in for anything that represented the Union. That included Catholics. That included this university that almost represents Catholicism. Then they threw him out,"

Claire paused for a second. "So, if he was so anti-Catholic, why did he come here in the first place?"

The three of us just thought about it in silence.

"Maybe he became, as they say, radicalized here somehow," I said.

"How could he have gotten radicalized here? The place is filled with ultra-conservative Catholics, devout liberal Catholics, and lazy Catholics. Where would the radicalization types come from?" Link said.

"There are always pockets. It is sometimes what makes them attractive. Different people, different thoughts," Claire said.

"I didn't know anyone else like Blake here. His rally, if you call it that, was just him. Students booed him and threw garbage at him," I said.

"Maybe that's just what he wanted," Claire said.

"I don't get it," I said.

"Martyrdom. A lot of the Lost Cause South bullshit is centered around persecution from the North. Blake killed himself, maybe because of it." Claire looked at me and kicked the dirt in front of her like she was trying to think.

"Where did Blake go after Notre Dame?" Claire asked. We both looked at her not knowing where she was going. She took out her phone.

"Hey, I know this is crazy, but where did Blake go to school after he left Notre Dame-if he went anywhere?"

She waited.

"You're fucking kidding me." She took the phone from her mouth and looked at us.

"He went to Mercer."

"Mercer?" I repeated. "Where Lacey is from?"

"The whack job conservative minister?" Link said.

"Maybe he and Blake were late-night buddies. Maybe Blake took Lacey's conservative shit and made it his own." Link looked at me and then Claire and then back to me. "I'm going to want to talk to him."

Graziano, the federal cop Link had sparred with, approached us. He was by himself.

"Thanks for taking care of this," he said in a perfunctory style. "The bureau appreciates all the help. You have an excellent force, Captain. We're happy to take it from here."

"You going to execute the evacuation plan?" Link said.

"Like I said, Captain, we will take it from here." He smiled while his mirrored shades hid his eyes.

"Fuck you and your fucking patronizing. Are you going to evacuate?"

Graziano turned and walked toward the cemetery exit.

We didn't waste any time getting to Lacey's office in O'Shag. Sure, it was the Saturday of the biggest football game of the year, but something told me this old hard-on of a minister wasn't a fan.

The four of us trotted to the entrance and climbed to the third floor. His office was 308, and as expected, he was there-pale skin, wire-rimmed glasses, buttoned-up collar, slicked-back hair, and long, thin fingers. He was hunched over a large textbook, yellow highlighter in hand.

"I beg your pardon," he said, his voice full of indignation. "This is a private office, and I am working. Please turn around and go back to where you came from."

"Look, Reverend, I know I'm supposed to shake in my boots when a man of the cloth scolds me, but I'm not an eight-year-old altar boy getting ready for Mass. I'm the captain of campus police, and I need to know some things," Link said. The intensity was back-the kind that could burn through drywall.

Jo stood at the doorway, expressionless.

"The nerve! Who do you think you are, talking to me like this? I will be speaking to your vice president," Lacey said, sitting back in his chair, puffed up with righteousness.

"Hey, Rev, save it for your sermon. Blake-tell us about Blake. I don't have a lot of time, and the stakes are too high to screw around with you right now," Link snapped.

"How dare you talk to a man of God like that! Show some respect!"

Link walked around the desk and grabbed Lacey by the neck.

I was pretty sure Lacey wasn't used to this kind of treatment.

"You were Blake's mentor. I know you were. What was your mission? There's a chance someone's going to blow up that stadium filled with people. I'll go to confession later today for this, but tell me about Blake!"

Lacey started to gasp, and I began to worry.

"Link..." I said softly.

He broke the hold.

Lacey exaggerated the gasp and threw his head down on his desk. "How dare you!" he croaked, his voice raspy.

"Yeah, I got that part, Lacey. Blake-tell me about Blake." Link wasn't letting up.

"Blake was a student. He deeply cared about theology. He cared about what was right. He hated the softening of scripture. He hated how Christianity was perverted to appease today's sinners. He is not alone."

"What does that mean?" I asked.

"There are many like him. Around the country, around the world-and yes, here at Notre Dame. Those seeking what is right."

"And the killings on this campus?" I said.

"I don't condone zealotry, but it is resonating. It's making a point. Maybe the blind will begin to see."

"What was his plan?" Link said.

"I-I-I..." Lacey stammered.

Link kicked the base of his chair, knocking it over.

"The plan, Lacey!" Link knelt beside him, six inches from his face. "This sinner doesn't care who you are. The plan!"

Lacey hesitated. Link punched him in the ribs. Lacey cried out, then whimpered.

"Blake hated football. He spoke of making it an example. He spoke of the South and Christianity finding redemption-on this blasphemous stadium and its obsession with a barbaric sport." He clutched his ribs and writhed.

"How?" Link shouted.

"I don't know!"

Link punched him in the ribs again.

"I swear! I swear! Don't hit me again!"

"Link, let's get to the stadium. Come on..." I said.

Link looked at me, then down at Lacey. He got up, and the three of us walked out in silence.

We crossed the quad and headed toward the stadium.

"I think there's confession immediately following the game - and before Mass in Alumni Hall," I said.

"Good to know," Link replied.

CHAPTER 19

Like 80,000 others, we were heading to the stadium to see the game. Unlike the others, we had a little more on our minds than whether the Irish could get the passing game going on Georgia's secondary or whether we could stop the run on defense.

Unfortunately, we didn't know what we were looking for, if anything at all. Our lead suspect was supposedly dead, the motive wasn't clear, and any methodology of terror or harm wasn't clear.

Other than that, we had everything under control.

If you've never been to a big Notre Dame home game or any major college football powerhouse, it is hard to explain. Maybe the soccer nuts in Europe might get it. Maybe not.

"Link, what are we looking for? In fact, what are we doing?" Claire said, not hiding her desperation very well.

"We have no official standing here. The Feds made that clear. Not sure what we could do even if we knew what was going on." Link wasn't happy.

"I guess it falls into the 'If you see something, say something,'" I said.

Claire stopped and looked at the south side of the monstrous stadium. People in blue and gold and green and people in red and gray were moving in all different directions. Bands were playing, and people were shouting "Go Irish! And Sic 'em!" The Viking parade band walked by with twice as many members as before. Co-eds in short green skirts and shiny gold sneakers and a group of students in head-to-toe gold body stockings sailed by on skateboards.

"Um, if you see something, say something..." Claire murmured.

"And to whom?" I said.

"We could go to the Falkenberg tailgater and drink bourbon," Link said. It was good to hear his humor return, as dark as it was. Then his phone pinged. I had gotten conditioned to have a stress reaction every time I heard it.

"Are you fucking kidding me? I'll be there in a second. C'momn Jo."

He was disconnected and just started shaking his head.

"The nut job fan, what's his name, Big Dog Earl or some shit? He's floating naked in St. Joe Lake, face down. No notes, no symbolism. Something else. Probably went for a drunken swim. I gotta go. You guys go to the game and keep an eye out. I'll be back on my stadium post as soon as I can."

Claire looked at me.

"Go Irish..." she said. "Doesn't feel right leaving him alone."

"He's a cop. It's what he does. This is something else, I think. Not what he needed, but it feels different."

"Jesus..." Claire said.

"Sic 'em..." I said. "Wanna go watch a football game?" The irony was intended.

She snickered. "Yeah, why not. It'll be fun watching your alma mater get their ass kicked."

The stadium lights were on in the twilight. We took our seats around the home forty, about 20 rows up next to the student section. Being a symposium guest had its perks. These were the best seats I'd ever had.

Georgia came out to a loud reception of boos. I elbowed Claire. Then, there was the familiar pause and the beginnings of what would build into deafening and energizing cheers. Coach Freeman, sporting one of his white quarter zips with the gold ND on his chest, appeared with the team behind him. He turned and yelled something intense at them. Then, he turned back around and led the team onto the field.

The band struck up the Fight Song, and the place went crazy. I never got tired of this.

I almost forgot what might be going on behind the scenes.

After the obnoxious TV timeout, "Here Come the Irish" stirred the crowd while our kicker teed it up. Then the Dropkick Murphys blasted *Shipping Up to Boston*, and the ball was in the air.

Who knows what was about to happen.

CHAPTER 20

It was the strangest way to experience something I usually really loved. Sure, all the pomp and circumstance was there, but it was poisoned by everything that was swirling around. I had so many conflicting emotions-dread, fear, and confusion. I'm sure Claire and Link felt it too.

Georgia was up 14, and it was only the second quarter. The Irish offense couldn't get anything going and seemed to have one three-and-out after another. Our punter was having a good day, which is never a great sign.

I texted Link, and he wrote back that Earl had drowned naked. Probably drunk. He was back at his post, and nothing was out of the ordinary. Yet.

Maybe we just misjudged the whole thing. Maybe the Feds knew what they were doing, and maybe we were three rookies who got carried away with each other's anxiety.

Blake was dead. So how do we explain the body on Rockne's grave? We weren't out of our minds. I just knew it.

"You're quiet," Claire said. "Is it because your team sucks, or is it the potential for a mass casualty incident that would kill 80,000 of your clan?"

"Actually, it would only be about 70,000 of my clan. There's probably 10,000 of yours here."

"True. There's solace in that," she said. There was a faint smile. "Pretty dark humor, huh?"

"Yeah." I looked at her. She smiled. "I don't know what other choice we have."

"Are those snipers?" Claire pointed her chin to the top of the press box. She turned and looked at each scoreboard. "There too. And there."

"Well, maybe the Feds took some precautions after all."

On cue, Leonard Jefferson picked off a Georgia pass and ran it 65 yards back for a touchdown. It got us on our feet and got, well, just me, cheering.

"Well, we may be facing Armageddon, but at least we'll cover the spread." Another one of my attempts at humor.

Nothing from Link.

No sign of extra law enforcement presence.

Nothing.

I still felt anxious as hell.

The Irish held Georgia in the next series, and as was the new strategy all over football, the Dawgs went for it on fourth down. We held and took over on downs.

On the very next play, our quarterback hit his favorite target in the end zone. The extra point was good, and the game was tied. Usually, this would make me ecstatic.

It didn't.

The halftime show featured the Irish marching band doing a tribute to Elvis Presley's 50th anniversary of playing the Joyce Center. As much as I love The King, the marching band versions of "Burning Love," "Hound Dog," "Suspicious Minds," and "Can't Help Falling in Love" just fell flat. The fight song closed the set, and that changed the crowd's reaction.

Georgia got the ball to start the half, and the kickoff was returned 98 yards for a touchdown. It was the sort of momentum killer that gave me a sick feeling in my gut.

During the subsequent TV timeout, a guy in a Georgia jacket and wearing red from head to toe marched out onto the field. When I say marched, I mean marched-he was being very formal. Stadium security was being a bit tentative in stopping him.

He was carrying a Confederate flag, and he marched to the interlocking ND in the center of the field. He then forcefully planted it in the heart of the symbol. He looked familiar.

"It's that ass, Big Earl, but it can't be..." Claire said, her voice trailing off.

Same outfit, same hairdo, same flag, but it just couldn't be.

The crowd greeted him with a chorus of boos, with a smattering of cheers coming from the Georgia section.

He was shouting. It was hard to make out.

Something about the South...something about burning, revenge, reckoning...

Security tackled him and escorted him off. A guard took the Confederate flag with them.

He was shouting the whole time he was escorted. It sounded like he kept repeating the same thing. It was hard to make out.

"What's he saying?" I asked Claire.

She squinted and turned her head.

"Burning, revenge, and reckoning?" Claire repeated.

I just looked at her.

"Fire was on every note at every murder scene," I said.

"There's something else," Claire said. I didn't let her finish. "Let's get to Link."

CHAPTER 21

"Let's go!" I said.

Claire and I fought our way through the middle of the row, past annoyed Irish fans unhappy first with their team losing and second with two fans interrupting their game early in the third quarter.

We both ran up to the exit and then as fast as we could to the end zone entrance and Gate One. Claire clearly was a runner, and we ran shoulder to shoulder. We had to dodge the beer and bathroom lines as we hit full sprint.

We neared the gate, and there was a line of ushers and security guards blocking the area. Paramedics were on the ground with what looked like two bodies, both in yellow security jackets. They were working fast, and even from this distance, seemed to be desperate.

Link and Jo ran up behind us and moved into the circle. He spoke on the walkie-talkie. He was surveying the area, and I could tell he was triaging everything in front of him.

The ambulances on site, meant for athletes, not security guards, pulled into the tunnel, and the two guards were quickly loaded in along with the paramedics working on them.

I called to Link.

He gave me a nod and waved me in, calling to the ushers to make room.

"He shot both of the security officers, then took off onto the campus," he said. "I've got campus police looking for him. The state police are on it, and of course, our friends the Feds are here as well. I'm going out there. You want to come?" Link said.

"Hell yeah," I said. I looked at Claire.

"I'm in," she said.

By now, the snow had started to fall, and a coating had begun to stick to the grass.

"Do we know what direction he went?" I asked.

"No," Link said without looking at me.

"Do we know where he's likely to go?" Claire asked.

"No," Link just kept moving.

"Do we have a plan?" I said.

"No," Link said.

We went past the library, past the engineering building, and headed toward the law school. Our steady trot seemed to be what was required, but at the same time, it seemed pointless.

We were coming up on Alumni Hall by the Gargoyle entrance.

Something dawned on me.

I stopped before the dormitory, right in line with the Golden Dome.

"What?" Link said with just a hint of annoyance.

"The tunnels," I said. Link looked at me. Claire raised an eyebrow. Jo stood off to the side.

"He knows about the tunnels. We saw that at Zahm. The campus is crawling with law enforcement. If he just disappeared, he might have gone underground," I said.

"Hell, why not? Let's go in through the Alumni entrance."

Link used his fob to get us in, and we ran the first floor to the staircase and went down to the basement level, past the food sales room and the trash chute, and across from the party room. Link produced a key and got us in.

The immediate temperature change and dampness fell over us. The dim lighting framed everything and made the atmosphere as creepy as the experience was. We ran a few hundred feet until we reached a crossroads.

"It would probably make sense to split up so we can cover more ground. The only thing is I'm the only one that's armed," Link said, and I could tell he was running that concept through his head.

"We won't approach him. If we find him, we'll call. How can you tell where you are down here?"

"The numbers on the wall give you a location. Jo, go with them so I know where you all are. You spot him, you call me with the number," Link said.

I nodded.

"Let's go. Be careful," Link said.

CHAPTER 22

Claire, Jo and I split at the junction-Link went left, we went right. The tunnel sloped upward and away from Alumni, concrete and damp beneath our feet, the air cooler and heavy with the smell of earth and rust.

We kept a steady trot, scanning walls, ceilings, alcoves-anything out of place. It didn't take long for my confidence to curdle into doubt. This was a maze, and we were guessing.

We reached another cross passage.

"Left or right?" Claire asked.

"Right." Jo interjected.

We went right without hesitation.

Less than a hundred feet in, Claire stopped abruptly.

Claire's iphone flashlight beam drifted up the wall as we walked, catching wet concrete, rusted brackets, old stains—tunnel history.

Then she stopped so suddenly I almost bumped into her.

"Trace," she said.

"What?"

She raised the light higher. "Look."

At first I didn't see anything. Just a seam in the concrete near the ceiling line, a run of conduit, the kind of utility junk you stop noticing after five minutes underground.

Then the beam caught it.

A small white disc—about the size of a silver dollar—stuck high on the wall like it belonged there.

Except it didn't.

A tiny LED winked on and off. Slow. Patient.

Like a heartbeat.

Claire's voice tightened. "Is that… wiring?"

"It's something," I said. "And it's new."

Jo stepped forward before either of us could say another word. She didn't look scared. She looked like a scientist approaching a beaker.

"That is not wiring," she said softly.

I glanced at her. "You know what it is?"

Jo nodded once. "It is a node."

Claire blinked. "A node?"

Jo lifted her own phone light and swept it down the tunnel. She didn't wave it wildly. She moved it with purpose—left wall, right wall, ceiling, corners—like she was searching for a pattern she already believed existed.

Twenty feet ahead, another identical disc flashed in the dark.

Then another.

My stomach sank.

Jo looked back at us, calm as a lab instructor.

"It is a Bluetooth mesh," she said. "They are placed like stepping stones. One speaks to the next."

Claire swallowed. "So… we're inside it."

Jo's eyes stayed on the blinking light above us.

"Yes," she said. "We are walking through the path."

I felt the tunnel tighten around us, even though the walls didn't move.

"Link went the other way," Claire whispered.

Jo nodded, already turning her flashlight forward again.

"Then we must move faster," she said. "Because whoever built this… did not build it for nothing."

The blinking nodes became our breadcrumbs.

Every twenty feet or so, another small white disc high on the wall. Another faint heartbeat of light. It was too consistent to be accidental. Too deliberate to be maintenance.

Claire kept her flashlight angled upward, jaw clenched. I could tell she wanted to say something—wanted to ask how any of this could be real—but the tunnels had a way of turning questions into wasted oxygen.

Jo didn't waste anything.

She moved with purpose now, almost faster than Link had been, and that alone told me how serious this was. Jo didn't rush. Jo calculated.

We followed the nodes through a bend, then another, deeper into the campus's underworld. The air grew colder. The ceiling dropped slightly. The concrete changed texture, newer in places, older in others, like the tunnel itself had scars.

Jo stopped again.

Not sudden this time. Certain.

She turned her flashlight in a slow circle and lifted it to the ceiling.

Then she whispered, almost reverent.

"We are under it."

Claire frowned. "Under what?"

Jo didn't look at her. She looked up as if she could see through forty feet of earth and stone.

"The Golden Dome," she said.

The words hit me wrong. Not because I didn't believe her.

Because I did.

I felt it then—the weight above us, the idea of it. The Dome wasn't just a building. It was a promise. A symbol. A thing you didn't touch.

Jo's voice sharpened.

"This is why the mesh is here," she said. "This is not random. This is a pathway."

Claire's eyes widened. "A pathway to what?"

Jo turned to me. "To deliver a command."

A command.

A simple word. A small thing.

The kind of small thing that could destroy something huge.

We moved again, slower now, like we were walking into a dangerous room.

The tunnel opened into a wider junction with pipes overhead, a metal cabinet bolted to the wall and old utility panels like.

And there he was.

Jeffrey Davis stood near a makeshift work area, half-hidden behind a concrete pillar. A portable light cast harsh shadows on his face. A small case sat open beside him—tools, batteries, connectors, things that looked harmless until you realized nothing down here was harmless.

In his hand was a phone.

His posture was calm. Not startled. Not surprised.

Like we were late.

"Trace Curran," he said, voice smooth, almost warm. "And Claire Bennett. And…"

His eyes moved to Jo, measuring her like a new variable.

"…a child."

Jo didn't flinch.

Davis smiled, the kind of smile that belonged on a pulpit.

"The fire is about to come," he said. "It makes us all honest."

Claire stepped forward, anger breaking through pain and fear like a blade.

"You killed Earl. You still are wearing his clothes. It is how you got access," she said.

"Ahh, the doctor has figured it out. Unfortunately it is too late. It is time for reckoning, retribution and revenge." He reached around to his back and produced a gun.

He lifted the phone slightly, He was as casual as a man checking the time.

"This place was built on faith," he said. "And faith always demands a reckoning." He paused. This was a presentation and we were his audience. "You will die in the fire if you don't die here first."

Claire glanced at me briefly. Then she spoke to Davis.

"You're a piece of racist shit. You are an embarrassment

to the South and the Confederacy." Again a quick glance at me. "You are an impostor, a charlatan. An embarrassment."

Claire was goading him. She was distracting him.

I felt Jo shift beside me—her attention not on Claire's words, but on the wall behind Davis. On the nodes. On the layout.

She was already mapping the system.

Davis continued, voice sliding into that double-meaning cadence preachers use when they want you to hear two messages at once.

"Fire is not destruction," he said. "Fire is cleansing. Fire is truth."

Claire barked a laugh, sharp and ugly.

"Oh, spare us," she said. "You're going to burn the Dome and call it salvation? That's your big masterpiece? A tantrum with explosives?"

For the first time, Davis's smile faltered.

Not because she was wrong.

Because she was effective.

His eyes hardened. His hand tightened on the phone.

"You don't understand," he said quietly. "This campus has lived too long in gold and denial."

Claire took another step, fearless in the worst possible way.

"No," she said. "You don't understand. You're nothing. You're a footnote with a grudge."

Davis's face went still.

And then he raised the gun hand. He fired.

Claire jerked as if someone had yanked her backward by the collar. Her mouth opened in shock. Her hand went to her shoulder.

"Claire!" I shouted.

She stumbled, hit the wall, slid down.

"Now, she'll shut her goddam mouth!" Davis yelled.

I didn't wait.I lunged at him with everything I had inside me.

Davis twisted, bringing the gun toward me—but my shoulder hit his chest and drove him into the concrete pillar. His arm snapped sideways. The gun barked again, the shot cracking into the ceiling.

His phone flew from his hand.

It hit the ground and skittered away, spinning in the dust.

Davis shoved me back with surprising strength, eyes wild now, mask gone.

"You can't stop it," he hissed. "You're already too late."

I saw the gun come up again.

Then a second sound tore through the tunnel. This one louder and harder on the ears.

Davis's body jolted.

His expression changed, not fear exactly—more disbelief, like the universe had broken its own rules.

He turned slightly.

And Link stepped out of the darkness behind him like a man the tunnel had created.

Link fired again.

Davis dropped.

The tunnel swallowed the sound after a beat, and for a second all I could hear was my own breathing and Claire's ragged gasp against the wall. Her shirt was now soaked in a dark crimson.

Link kept his weapon trained on Davis until he was sure.

"He's dead," Link said.

Then he looked at me.

"You okay?"

I nodded, barely.

My eyes went to Claire. "Claire's been shot."

"I'm here," she rasped. "I'm… here. I'm okay. Its bleeding but I'm okay."

Jo had moved without anyone noticing.

She was crouched near the Davis's fallen phone.

Her hand hovered over it but didn't touch it.

Her voice cut through the moment.

"Stop."

Link took a step forward. "Jo—"

"No," she said, sharper now. "No one moves."

The tunnel went still.

Link froze mid-step.

I held my breath.

Claire stared at Jo like she was seeing her for the first time.

Jo's eyes stayed on the phone, unblinking.

"If you move fast," she said, "you may trigger the wrong thing."

Link frowned. "The phone's just a phone."

Jo shook her head.

"The phone ignites the mesh," she said. "It is the equivalent of a detonator."

I swallowed. "Explain."

Jo finally reached down and picked up the phone—carefully, like it was a live animal.

She angled the screen toward us.

A timer glowed bright and merciless:

00:55

And counting down.

Claire whispered, "What is that?"

Jo's voice stayed calm, but her hands were steady in a way that made my blood run colder.

"This is not a bomb timer," she said. "It is a signal timer."

Link's jaw clenched. "Meaning what?"

"It means," Jo said, "in fifty-five seconds, the message will be sent through the mesh."

She lifted her flashlight and pointed it down the tunnel behind Davis.

"The nodes," she said. "They repeat the command. One speaks to the next. The next speaks again."

Her eyes flicked upward to the ceiling line where another small disc blinked.

"Like people passing a message," she said. "But the message is detonation."

The timer rolled down:

00:47… 00:46…

Link started forward again, controlled but urgent. "Then we smash the nodes. We—"

Jo snapped her head toward him.

"No," she said.

Link stopped.

Jo's voice softened, but it didn't lose authority.

"This is for me to do, Captain. Back up please."

The man in me wanted to argue. The man in me wanted to protect her. The part of me that had watched her move through the tunnels like she belonged there understood something else:

Jo was the only one who could do this without making it worse.

She handed the phone to me without taking her eyes off the wall.

"Do not touch anything," she said. "Do not press anything."

I held it like it was a Tiffany vase.

Jo stepped toward the nearest node, high on the wall. She didn't climb or scramble. She reached into her pocket and pulled out a small tool—something simple, functional, the kind of thing a work-study student might carry without anyone thinking twice.

She studied the node for one second. Then she looked down at the timer reflected faintly on the phone screen in my hands.

00:34

Jo spoke, not to us now, but to the system.

"If I remove the wrong piece," she said quietly, "the command may reroute."

Link's voice was tight. "How do you stop it?"

Jo's eyes narrowed.

"I break the path," she said. "I cut the chain." She was talking to her self."

She reached up and pressed her fingers along the edge of the disc, finding the seam.

00:22

Claire whispered, "Jo…"

Jo didn't answer.

She twisted—precise, controlled.

The disc loosened.

A tiny LED blinked faster, like it knew it was dying.

Jo's hand moved again—one clean motion.

The node came free.

The tunnel lights flickered once.

A deep hum vibrated through the concrete, like the building itself had felt something change.

Then—

Silence.

The beeping stopped.

I stared down at the phone. The string of nodes lost their LED lights.

The timer froze.

00:09

Frozen.

Not detonated.

Just... dead.

Jo exhaled once, slow.

Link finally moved, stepping in close, weapon still up, eyes scanning for anything else.

"Is it over?" he asked.

Jo held the node in her hand and stared at it..

Then she looked at Link. She didn't smile and for the longest time she didn't say anything. A single tear ran down her cheek.

She began to speak. She didn't look at any of us.

"This university is everything to me. This university gave me, my family hope." More tears ran down her face that she didn't acknowledge. "I could not let him desecrate

Our Lady." Her face contorted as she felt but didn't acknowledge the tears.

"You saved our lives," Claire said. It came out simply and with authenticity.

"You saved us, you saved Our Lady, you saved this university," I said. I felt my voice crack.

"Jo you saved our lives," Link said. "You saved Our Lady, our university."

"This university saved me." She said without looking at us.

Jo looked at the three of us. She wiped her eyes and sniffed back the remnants of her tears. A small, very small smile cracked and after a moment she looked at the three of us.

We all instinctfully went to her and hugged her. She held on tight and let loose crying. It went on for a long moment and then she broke it off.

She whipped the tears from her eyes and took a long cleansing breath before looking at us. Then she spoke.

"Go Irish," she said.

CHAPTER 23

Law enforcement of every shape and size was gathered around the entrance to the tunnel, which was just off to the right of the sidewalk outside the Administration Building. Our Lady and the Golden Dome remained intact.

The paramedics got Claire bandaged up and reassured us that it was a soft tissue flesh wound and that she would probably spend the night at St. Joseph's Medical Center. She was talking, and maybe more importantly, laughing by the time they got her in the ambulance.

Garcia, the fed, came over to us while we were talking with six of the campus police and a few of the South Bend uniforms.

"I saw the setup in the tunnel. I owe you an apology," Garcia said and extended his hand. Link shook it and nodded. He didn't say anything. "We're bringing the forensic team down there now. You're welcome to join us," Garcia said.

Link seemed to mull that over.

"I'll pass, but I'd love to see your reports," Link said.

"Of course, Captain," Garcia said. Then he and his team climbed down the manhole to do their thing.

Link waited a few beats until he knew they were out of earshot.

"Fuck them," he said with a laugh.

Just then, the stadium erupted. Fireworks shot off the top of the stadium.

Public address announcer Chris Ackles

shouted, "Jeter's field goal is good! The Irish win in triple overtime 34-31!" The crowd noise and the Victory March were deafening.

"Pretty good day for the Irish," I said.

Link laughed and slapped me on the back.

"You're going to be even more of a legend than you already are," I said.

He smiled and shook his head.

"Something tells me this won't make the cover of *Notre Dame Magazine* or *The Observer*. Hell, the administration doesn't even list the drunk arrests on a football weekend."

"Probably," I said. "Wanna get a beer? Morris Inn?"

"Why not," Link said. "Jo, you want to join us?"

"I have to get to the library," She smiled and headed in that direction.

"That's quite a work-study student you got there," I said.

"Uh-huh," Trace said and slapped me on the back.

CHAPTER 24

After a few hours of drinking and revelry with a bunch of people who had far less to celebrate than we did, Link and I, exhausted, called it a night.

First, I texted Claire.

"You accepting visitors?"

Fifteen minutes later.

"Unfortunately, no. I'm doped up. Going to sleep. Doing fine. They say I can fly out tomorrow."

Damn, I had forgotten my flight back was tomorrow at 10 from Midway.

"I won't get to see you. My flight is first thing in the morning."

I had poured myself a bourbon, and my eyes were closing.

A half an hour went by, and a ping woke me up.

"Go Irish! You can buy a pizza from me anytime."

It made me smile.

"I'd want to keep you on my porch." I texted back.

"Sic 'em!" She signed off.

CHAPTER 25

I went back home and to the bar on Wednesday. Stocking the coolers boredom was quite welcome, and it was good to have Rocky's company. His yawns and full-body collapses were soothing.

"You're back!" It was 12:01, and that meant George. "What a game! What a game!"

"Yessir. Great to be there for it," I said.

"Man, how were the seats?"

"Great!" I said with as much enthusiasm as I could muster. Just then, my phone pinged.

"Excuse me, George. I have to answer this." George put his hands up in a "No Problem" gesture.

It was from Claire.

I found out it's a home-and-home schedule. I say you come down here next fall. Pizza's on me.

I smiled.

You got it. I texted back.

"Anyway, what a game! I knew the Irish would pull it out." George didn't miss a beat.

"Yessir!" I said.
"Had everyone sweating right up to the end!"
I smiled at George.
"That's for sure." I couldn't stop smiling. "Go Irish!"

The End

ABOUT THE AUTHOR

TOM SCHRECK is the author of Amazon's #1 hard-boiled mystery, *The Vegas Knockout*. He counts Robert B. Parker, John D. MacDonald, JA Konrath, Reed Farrel Coleman, Ken Bruen and Michael Connelly among his favorite crime fiction authors and his Duffy Dombrowski series has been referred to as "As good or better as the early Spenser." He is a columnist with Westchester Magazine and a frequent contributor to Crimespree Magazine, Referee, and other publications.

Follow Tom and Subscribe to updates at
TomSchreck.com

BOOKS BY TOM SCHRECK

<u>The Duffy Dombrowski Mysteries</u>

On the Ropes

TKO

Out Cold

The Vegas Knockout

The Ten Count

The Comeback

The Shuffle

The Real Deal

The Split Decision

Getting Dunn

Redeeming Trace